A Vow for the Viscount

Barrington's Brigade
Book 4

Ruth A. Casie

ARE YOU SIGNED UP FOR DRAGONBLADE'S BLOG?

You'll get the latest news and information on exclusive giveaways, exclusive excerpts, coming releases, sales, free books, cover reveals and more.

Check out our complete list of authors, too!

No spam, no junk. That's a promise!

Sign Up Here

www.dragonbladepublishing.com

Dearest Reader;

Thank you for your support of a small press. At Dragonblade Publishing, we strive to bring you the highest quality Historical Romance from some of the best authors in the business. Without your support, there is no 'us', so we sincerely hope you adore these stories and find some new favorite authors along the way.

Happy Reading!

CEO, Dragonblade Publishing

Additional Dragonblade books by Author Ruth A. Casie

Barrington's Brigade Series
A Marriage for the Marquess (Book 1)
A Dilemma for the Duke (Book 2)
A Redemption for the Baron (Book 3)
A Vow for the Viscount (Book 4)

The Ladies of Sommer-by-the-Sea Series
The Lady and Her Quill (Book 1)
The Lady and the Spy (Book 2)
The Lady and Her Duke (Book 3)
The Duke's Lost Love (Novella)

Pirates of Britannia Series
Donald
Hugh
Graham
The Pirate's Jewel
The Pirate's Redemption

The Lyon's Den Series
The Lyon's Gambit
The Lyon's Alliance

Chapter One

MARY-ANN SEATON HAD always liked the front parlor in the late morning. The tall windows caught the sun just right and filled the room with a soft warmth that dulled the sharp edges of her thoughts. This morning, the golden light spilled across the room, which had been transformed into a private fitting room. The usual furniture had been rearranged to accommodate fabrics, gowns, and pins, while the scent of lavender beeswax, and floral Darjeeling tea hung in the air.

Mary-Ann stood in front of the full-length cheval mirror, the hem of her nearly finished wedding gown pooled in soft folds around her feet. Her auburn hair had been swept back loosely for the fitting, a few tendrils falling over her shoulder. Her expression, reflected in the glass, was calm. Peaceful. Even quietly pleased.

She turned slightly as Mrs. Pembroke, the dressmaker, circled her, pinning fabric and murmuring to herself as she worked.

Finally, done. She stood back and took in Mary-Ann. "He'll be stunned when he sees you," the seamstress said with a warm smile.

Mary-Ann tilted her head and gazed into the mirror. "That is my plan."

The gown was lovely, a rose gold satin with delicate ivory trim at the neckline, and sleeves that fluttered just off her shoulders. It was everything she had imagined. It was refined. Graceful. Entirely hers.

Across the room, seated in a high-backed chair near the hearth, Mrs. Bainbridge watched with an appraising eye and a small, fond smile. She had arrived an hour ago under the pretense of keeping Mary-Ann company during the fitting, though her glances toward the window had grown more frequent.

Mary-Ann had once been a student at the Sommer-by-the-Sea Female Seminary, where Mrs. Bainbridge, the founder and headmistress, had encouraged her, boldly and against all expectations, to pursue mathematics and finance. Their acquaintance had grown into a bond far deeper than one of headmistress and pupil. Mary-Ann trusted her implicitly.

"Are you comfortable, Mrs. Bainbridge?" she asked, catching her guest's reflection in the mirror. "You've seemed a bit unsettled since you arrived."

Mrs. Pembroke motioned her to turn.

Mrs. Bainbridge started, then gave a light chuckle. "Forgive me. I'm distracted, I suppose. It's not every day a woman accepts a marriage proposal and then spends the week pretending she hasn't."

Mrs. Pembroke froze, her mouth forming a perfect 'O,' t.

Mary-Ann spun around sharply, the satin hem whispering across the carpet. "You accepted Lord Barrington!" she said, unable to contain her excitement.

"I did," Mrs. Bainbridge replied, pouring herself a cup of tea.

"You didn't say a word!"

"Well, he looked so determined. As if I'd regret it more if I said no. It was last Saturday. This time, he had that look about him, as though he'd draft a treaty if I refused to give him a clear answer."

Mary-Ann grinned. "That sounds exactly like him. I suppose he prepared a written proposal, thoroughly footnoted." Mary-Ann attempted a solemn expression, but failed miserably. "Citing at least three reasons why he was the best candidate."

"Yes, well," Mrs. Bainbridge said, her eyes crinkling as she passed up the sugar bowl, "he did offer footnotes. I've never been one to be bullied into anything. Not even marriage."

"And yet you said yes."

"The man is rather persuasive. And, between us, it's rather nice to be admired so… stubbornly."

Mrs. Pembroke found her voice again and smiled. "Congratulations, Mrs. Bainbridge. That is wonderful news."

"Thank you, Mrs. Pembroke." Mrs. Bainbridge lifted her chin a bit. "I thought you may have guessed my secret when I was in your shop earlier this week."

"I did have my suspicions, but I knew you would let us know when you were ready. His lordship is a wonderful man." The seamstress went back to work.

"Now I understand why you haven't stopped smiling," Mary-Ann teased. She had once been a student at the Sommer-by-the-Sea Female Seminary, which Mrs. Bainbridge founded. She had always admired her former teacher and headmistress's blend of grace and grit. It was Mrs. Bainbridge who had encouraged her talent for finance and mathematics. They were odd talents for a young lady, perhaps, but ones that Mary-Ann had cultivated into sharp instincts and a rare understanding of her father's shipping business.

"And yet you said yes."

Mrs. Bainbridge's eyes softened. "Yes. And I don't regret it. Between us, it's rather lovely to be admired so… stubbornly."

Mary-Ann's smile faltered, just for a moment.

She turned back to the mirror, letting the conversation drift away as Mrs. Pembroke resumed her careful work. The gown shimmered faintly in the light, its delicate trim catching the sun. It was perfect. Just as it should be. Just as everything was supposed to be.

And yet…

That quiet voice inside her, the one she'd learned to ignore, stirred.

"Have you told anyone else?" Mary-Ann asked.

Mrs. Bainbridge shook her head. "Not yet. Though I daresay,

half the village will know by sundown. I believe his lordship sent a notice to the London Gazette as well as the Sommer Sentinel. We all know how London and Sommer-by-the-Sea thrive on gossip." She took a sip of tea.

"Will the wedding be here or in London?"

"That," Mrs. Bainbridge said with a sigh, "is already a matter of debate. I thought here, for simplicity's sake. Barrington is discussing the event with me as if it were a military operation. He mentioned his family's tradition of large weddings. Personally, at this point, Gretna Green sounds good to me."

Mary-Ann chuckled. "You know you don't mean that. I believe your Lord Barrington enjoys showing you off just as much as you enjoy being seen on his arm. I've seen your face light up when he enters a room."

"I suppose I must be more careful to control my feelings, especially around you."

"I don't think you can." Mary-Ann shook her head and tried not to smile.

"Excuse me, Miss Mary-Ann. One final turn, please," Mrs. Pembroke asked.

Mary-Ann executed a grand sweeping turn and let the skirt fall around her.

"Yes," Mrs. Pembroke nodded, "the length and weight are perfect."

"Mrs. Bainbridge, have you chosen your gown?" Mary-Ann nodded to the dressmaker, pleased as she was.

"Not yet. I'm torn between two gowns. One makes me feel like a duchess. The other makes me feel like myself. Naturally, I've chosen neither."

Mary-Ann grinned. "Then you're waiting for a third to appear to help you make a decision?"

"Or for a modiste to invent one that satisfies both sides of my nature." She gave Mrs. Pembroke a wink.

"If you crave a diplomatic gown," Mrs. Pembroke said while she gathered her pins, "I will gladly create one for you."

"I wouldn't have anyone else create a gown for me." Mrs. Bainbridge took another sip of tea. "I'm in no hurry. We haven't decided on a date for the wedding yet. That appears to be another negotiation."

They shared another laugh. The moment stretched comfortably while the dressmaker packed up her things.

"Rodney," Mary-Ann murmured, the name barely above a breath.

Rodney Wilkinson was a good man. Kind. Steady. Thoughtful in a way that made her feel cherished, seen. He listened with quiet sincerity and never sought to impress. Their courtship had been proper and patient, marked by gentle laughter, shared goals, and a quiet understanding that had deepened over time.

Their life together would be calm. Respectable. Safe.

She smiled faintly and adjusted the sleeve of her gown. It would be a good match, better than most, by any measure. She was proud of the choice she had made.

Still, the smallest ripple of doubt stirred, not about him, never about him, but about herself.

Would she be a good wife? Would she know what to say, what to do, how to be enough for a man like Rodney? Could she make him happy, truly happy, beyond duty and affection?

She drew a breath, letting it out slowly. It was a solemn moment. No wonder her hands trembled.

The sound of muffled voices in the foyer reached their ears, an urgent male voice, low and sharp. It sounded like a commotion until a loud crash, followed by Mr. Hollis, the butler's voice.

Mary-Ann frowned. "Did someone—?"

The dressmaker straightened. "Shall I see what's amiss?"

But Mary-Ann was already moving. She slipped from the small, raised platform, her slippers silent against the carpet, the gown rustling around her legs. She crossed the parlor, opened the door, and entered the hall just as another voice, low unmistakable, cut through the air.

Her heart stopped.

For a moment, it was as if the world had narrowed to a single, impossible sound. It couldn't be. And yet her feet moved of their own accord as if her body had recognized what her mind still refused to believe. The echo of his voice struck like a memory made real. He stood in front of her thinner, his shoulders slightly stooped, his travel-worn coat dusted from the road. His dark brown hair was longer now, touched with silver at the temples. And his face, so familiar it hurt, was pale, drawn, but unmistakably his.

Quinton Hollingsworth. Viscount Rockingham.

Alive. Her knees weakened, and for a moment, she forgot how to breathe.

He looked up, and their eyes met.

Everything else fell away. She reached instinctively for the edge of the doorframe, steadying herself as her heart stumbled, her breath caught, and for a moment, the years collapsed inward.

Her voice, when it came, was barely more than a whisper.

"I thought I'd never see you again."

Chapter Two

MARY-ANN DID NOT remember crossing the threshold into the hall. Her feet seemed to move without her permission, the gown whispering behind her like a phantom. The marble, the filtered late morning light, everything had the texture of a half-remembered dream. Her limbs moved out of habit, but her mind remained suspended somewhere between disbelief and numb recognition. She could see him, yes, but her head wasn't able to decide what it meant. Her breath had shortened. Her pulse fluttered in her throat. This wasn't possible. And yet it was.

This wasn't possible.

And yet it was.

The world felt thin and muffled. Her heartbeat was louder than the voices around her. When she reached the hall, Quinton stood just in front of her, still and composed, like a man anchoring himself to a moment he hadn't dared to hope for.

"Mary-Ann," was all he said. His voice was roughened by disuse or distance, but the tone was unmistakably his.

She swallowed, her hand grasping her skirt. "You're really here."

Her knees weakened.

He moved quickly. His hands were suddenly on her arms, steady and real. She didn't resist. She couldn't even if she wanted to.

"Careful,' he said, his voice low.

She nodded, though her pulse was erratic and her vision

tinged with white at the edges. He was real. That was the part she couldn't grasp.

"I'm all right," she managed, though she wasn't certain it was true.

"Mary-Ann?" Mrs. Bainbridge's voice came from behind her.

"She needs to sit," Quinton said gently.

"Miss Seaton," Mr. Hollis said from the archway, his voice calm but purposeful. "Perhaps you'd be more comfortable in the drawing room."

Quinton looked to her for confirmation. She gave a faint nod.

He guided her gently down the hall and into the quieter space.

She let herself be led. Her steps moved, but her mind stayed behind—still trying to rewrite the moment he walked through the door.

The drawing room was cool and bright, the curtains pulled wide, the scent of beeswax lingering faintly beneath the floral arrangements. She sank onto the settee, her knees still weak.

The warmth of his touch lingered long after he let her go.

Her fingers found the folds of her skirt and held them tight.

Quinton stood just inside the doorway, his posture uncertain. He looked older—not only in the silver at his temples or the thinness of his face, but in the set of his shoulders. The man she remembered had been bright with laughter, capable of both sharp wit and quiet comfort. This man had been carved down to something quieter. A survivor.

And her heart ached.

"You're thinner," she said because her heart was pounding too fast to say what she meant.

His lips pulled back in a familiar smirk. "So are you. But you're still the only one I'd trust to say it out loud."

She flushed, not at the words, but at the memory of him, of them. They had once spoken easily and instinctively, finishing each other's thoughts, teasing and tender. Now there was only distance.

She wanted to ask him more, where had he been, what had he seen, but the words stuck behind the lump in her throat.

"How?" she asked. "No one, not the War Office, not the newspapers, no one knew."

He nodded slowly. "I was told that they tried. I was held… somewhere unofficial. Not by the French army. Something else. Something worse."

Her breath caught. "You were a prisoner?"

"Of sorts."

A shiver passed through her. There was a hollowness in his voice that frightened her more than his words.

She sat straighter, her hands in her lap, twisting the fabric of her gown. "And no one told us."

He looked away. "Perhaps, that was best. You wouldn't want to…" He didn't finish.

There was a long silence.

She studied him. "Where have you been, Quinton? What happened to you?"

"I've been in places I wouldn't wish on anyone," he said. "As soon as Barrington brought me back to England, I came here. I had to see you with my own eyes."

She rose and crossed to him slowly. "Of all the places you could have gone…"

He nodded. "I hadn't meant to arrive like this. I didn't plan it. But once I was back… I couldn't stay away. Barrington told me you were engaged." He drew a breath. "But I needed to see you."

"I thought you were dead," she whispered. "For so long, I thought… and then I had to stop. I had to go on."

He nodded again, silent.

She lifted her hand before she could think better of it, her fingers trembling as they hovered near his face. Slowly, reverently, she brushed her fingertips across his cheek. The bristle of his unshaven jaw, the warmth of his skin. It was real. He closed his eyes at her touch, and when he opened them again, he caught her hand in his. His grip was gentle but firm. Her breath stilled.

"You came back," she whispered.

"I told you I would," he replied. Not a boast, not a tease. Just the truth.

They stood there, suspended between the past and the present, heartbreak and possibility.

A knock interrupted them.

One of the maids stepped in, eyes wide with curiosity. "Pardon me, miss. Mrs. Bainbridge is in the hall. Shall I show her in?"

"Please do," Mary-Ann said quickly.

Mrs. Bainbridge entered, composed, her eyes flicking between them with unmistakable curiosity.

"Lord Rockingham," she said warmly. "What a surprise and a relief. Welcome home."

Quinton bowed slightly. "Thank you, Mrs. Bainbridge. It's good to be here."

"Do you plan to stay long?" she asked.

Quinton's response was quiet. "As long as I'm needed."

Before more could be said, another knock sounded.

The door opened, and Rodney Wilkinson entered, composed as ever, his expression schooled into a pleasant surprise.

"Mrs. Bainbridge." He turned toward Quinton. "Lord Rockingham," he said warmly. "Welcome home."

Quinton inclined his head. "Mr. Wilkinson."

"How fortunate that you've arrived now," Wilkinson continued. "There's so much to celebrate." He turned toward Mary-Ann. "I was on my way to your father. He mentioned a discrepancy in the quarter report." He gave her a hint of a smile. "I told him I'd sort it out for him."

Mary-Ann's stomach turned. That was her responsibility.

Quinton didn't flinch, but Mary-Ann saw it, the slightest stiffening.

"I'll take my leave." Quinton turned to Mrs. Bainbridge. "It was good seeing you, Mrs. Bainbridge."

"I'm so glad you've returned." Her eyes softened.

Mary-Ann took a step toward him. "Will you stay in Sommer-by-the-Sea long?"

He turned to her. "That depends," he said, his voice low. "But I won't be far."

"Quinton—" she began, but he was already turning.

He paused at the threshold and glanced back, his voice low and certain. "You look well, Mary-Ann, and strong."

The door clicked shut behind him.

She stood still, her heart thudding against her ribs. The ache that bloomed in her chest wasn't confusion. It was recognition.

She moved to a chair and sat.

Wilkinson lingered, his expression unreadable. He poured himself a glass of sherry from the sideboard.

"He doesn't look well," he said, swirling the sherry in his glass.

Mary-Ann glanced at Mrs. Bainbridge but didn't respond to him.

"No doubt he's had a… complicated journey," he added.

She looked up. "You make it sound like you know what happened."

"I know he was missing. And now he's not," Wilkinson said, lifting his glass slightly. "We should all be grateful for that."

She narrowed her eyes. "That doesn't sound like gratitude."

He offered a tight smile. "My apologies, Mary-Ann. I meant no offense."

She rose, suddenly aware she was still wearing her gown. "Please excuse me, Rodney. I need to change." She turned to Mrs. Bainbridge. "Will you help me, please?"

"Of course," came the reply.

Rodney bowed slightly. "Of course. You go on. I'll see myself out."

Mrs. Bainbridge offered her arm without hesitation. Together they crossed the room, their steps quiet over the carpet. Mary-Ann did not look back.

Rodney remained by the window, still holding the glass of sherry. He watched them go, the faint clink of the glass against his ring the only sound.

Then he drained it, set it aside, and followed the silence out.

Chapter Three

THE FOLLOWING MORNING, with mist along the rooftops, Mary-Ann's mind refused to stay in the present. She conjured up the last time she'd been with Quinton before he left for the Peninsula.

It had been early spring then, too. The cherry trees had just begun to bloom along the edge of Seaton Drive, and the breeze carried the scent of sea salt and wild thyme. He had arrived early, dressed in his regimentals, the gold buttons glinting beneath a gray sky. His horse fidgeted near the gate, sensing Quinton's tension. So had she.

"You're leaving now," she had said, trying not to let it sound like an accusation. Try as she may, her voice caught anyway.

"It's only a short mission." He had smiled, that half-smile that never quite hid the sharpness in his eyes. "I'll be back before you miss me.

She stepped closer, and his laughter quickly faded.

He was still, his expression softened as he looked down at her. He gently slipped his arms around her and drew her into his embrace.

She went to him without any resistance, resting her hands on the front of his coat, feeling the steady rise and fall of his breath and the firm line of his shoulder beneath her cheek.

"I'll miss you the moment you're gone," she whispered.

"I'll write every week," he promised. "Now, don't lose any of my letters," he added with a wry tilt of his head.

"I never lose letters," she said, defiant even then. "Why would I misplace something that matters to me more?"

He sobered at that, his hands lifting to cradle her face. His brow touched hers. "I love you, my Mary-Ann. Always remember that. I vow to you that when I come back, I'll make you my wife."

She'd nodded, too choked for words.

He kissed her. Not gently, not cautiously, but as if sealing his vow with something more permanent than paper. It was the kind of kiss that branded itself into memory. The kind that lived in the spaces between heartbeats. Her hands tightened in the front of his coat as her feet left the ground just slightly, as though the force of it lifted her. Time blurred. The scent of him, the heat, the certainty. Everything else fell away. It wasn't her first kiss. But it was the first that made her believe in forever.

And then, sharper than guilt, deeper than regret, came the sudden thought of Rodney. His quiet steadiness. His trust in her. The ring on her finger. What would he think if he knew what stirred in her heart now?

She hadn't meant to betray anything. Only to remember. But remembering felt like a betrayal all the same.

Mary-Ann's fingers touched her lips. She could still feel the pressure of his kiss, the promise that it held. He had mounted his horse, turned back once to tip his fingers in salute, and then he was gone down the lane, his red coat disappearing like a flag swallowed by the mist.

But yesterday's man was different. The fire that once blazed so brightly had tempered into something quieter and more deliberate. He had been tested, shaped by things he had not yet spoken aloud. The boyish laughter was gone, but in its place stood a man forged by experience. And somehow, that made him no less hers.

Quinton hadn't begged. He hadn't tried to reclaim her. And that unsettled her more than if he had. It left room for questions she wasn't ready to answer and feelings she had buried too deeply to ignore.

She thought of the way he looked at her, the way his hand had closed around hers like an anchor. If Mrs. Bainbridge hadn't appeared… would he have kissed her? And what unsettled her more was the quiet flutter in her chest at the thought.

She hadn't cried. She hadn't screamed. She had simply… stopped. As though the world narrowed to the space between them, and for a heartbeat, nothing else existed.

He was here. Not a dream, not a whisper of the past, but flesh and blood, and more than anything, he was real.

Relief struck her first, sharp and bright. Then came the confusion. And the ache.

Her fingers brushed the rose-gold satin gown hanging on her dressing screen. It was meant to mark a beginning. But now it felt as if she was suspended between two lives, one imagined, and one returned. The silk had been chosen for a future she no longer recognized. A future that now felt like someone else's dream.

She had changed into a soft morning gown, hoping the shift might settle her thoughts. But the silk still clung to her skin, not the fabric, but the memory.

She had not slept. Her mind churned with questions, her heart caught between memory and uncertainty. All night she had stared at the ceiling, trying to make sense of what had happened and what it meant that Quinton was here, dusty, hollow-eyed, standing beneath the chandelier like a ghost given flesh. That image refused to leave her.

For years, she had begged for a word. Letters, whispers, confirmation of life or death. Nothing came. And so she learned to stop asking. She trained herself to smile, to laugh again. To believe it was right to move forward. But yesterday, when she saw him, it was as if time had collapsed in on itself. As if the years he'd been away never happened.

Each time she closed her eyes, she saw his face. Worn, drawn, but still Quinton. The slope of his brow. The way he said her name, his voice roughened now, shadowed with experience.

It wasn't just that she had grieved him. She had loved him. And love like that did not vanish. She let out a deep breath. No, a love like theirs settled in the quiet parts of the soul and waited, even if she had convinced herself otherwise.

Rodney had never made her breath catch. She never found

herself reaching for him in dreams or seeing him in sunlight through the window. He had always been practical. Present. Polite. But love had never burned between them. It had only ever simmered, safe and subdued.

A knock broke her thoughts.

"Come in," she said, turning.

Mrs. Bainbridge entered with a quiet grace, carrying a tray. "Tea," she said. "I took this from Mrs. Aldridge, just outside your door." She set it on the small table by the chaise. "And company if you want it."

Mary-Ann offered her a tired smile. "Thank you. I think I do."

They sat together on the chaise, the porcelain clinking of teacups the only sound for a long moment. Mrs. Bainbridge passed her the cup as if it might offer answers. Mary-Ann wrapped her fingers around the warm cup to keep from fidgeting, but didn't drink. Her eyes remained fixed on the window, following the curl of white foam as waves met the shore below the cliffs.

A breeze stirred the hem of the curtain, and for the briefest moment, she remembered the feel of Quinton's greatcoat beneath her fingers, the rough wool warmed by his body, the scent of sea salt clinging to him even then. Her gaze drifted to the gulls wheeling above the distant sea. Her thoughts swirled like the tides, memories, what-ifs, and unspoken questions.

Mrs. Bainbridge did not push. She did not pry. She simply waited, offering presence rather than pressure.

"He's changed," Mary-Ann said softly. She didn't mean it as a complaint, only as a statement of fact.

"Of course he has," Mrs. Bainbridge replied gently. "You have, too."

Mary-Ann looked down at her tea. "He's… quieter but steadier somehow. Still tender. Still clever. But there is something locked away. Something I can't reach"

"Some men return shattered," Mrs. Bainbridge said gently. "Others return reshaped, hardened in places, softened in others. It sounds as though Captain Hollingsworth is still very much himself, just with more to carry than before."

Mary-Ann didn't speak for a long while. "I don't know how to feel. I should be furious. I waited so long… and then I stopped. I had to. There were days I told myself I was foolish for waiting and that I had wasted too much time already. When I stopped looking… I felt guilty. But also… I felt lighter. And now I regret that I didn't do more. Instead, I gave up. I let myself move on. And now…"

"And now your heart is remembering what your mind tried to forget."

Mary-Ann's lips parted, but she said nothing.

Mrs. Bainbridge's voice softened. "When I lost my husband, I told myself it was enough to survive. But surviving isn't living. It's only now, with Barrington, that I remember what it means to feel… awake."

Mary-Ann turned to her, eyes searching. "What do you think I should do?"

Mrs. Bainbridge stirred her tea slowly. "I think…" She paused, choosing her words. "I think you owe it to yourself to be certain. To ask the questions you're afraid to ask. If what you have with Mr. Wilkinson is built on comfort and convenience, then perhaps it isn't what your heart truly needs."

Mary-Ann looked away, her voice a murmur. "He's been so patient. So kind. Steady. Dependable."

"That speaks well of him," Mrs. Bainbridge said. "But kindness is not love. And patience is not passion."

Mary-Ann blinked, the words settling over her like the hush of a turning page, quiet, but full of meaning.

"You once told me Quinton made everything seem sharper. Like the world stood still when he looked at you. Do you still feel that, even after everything?"

Mary-Ann hesitated, then nodded slowly. "Yes. I didn't expect to. But yes."

"Then you have your answer. Not all of it, perhaps. But

enough to begin." She gave Mary-Ann a faint smile. "The rest will come. If it's meant to."

A silence stretched between them. Then Mary-Ann exhaled, long and slow.

"I'm glad he's alive and safe," she whispered. "Even if I haven't figured out what that means."

She had asked, in the drawing room. *Where had he been?* But his answers had only deepened the silence.

Part of her still ached to know more. What he had seen. What had broken in him. There was something in the spaces between his words that unsettled her more than anything he'd said aloud.

How did one rebuild a bridge that had vanished beneath the sea?

Mrs. Bainbridge reached over and gently squeezed her hand.

They didn't speak again. Not right away.

Outside, the sea breeze stirred the curtains, and the world beyond the window carried on as though nothing had changed.

But Mary-Ann knew better.

Everything had changed.

Chapter Four

THE SAME MORNING, across town, the sun barely pierced the lingering mist. Quinton stood motionless, on the narrow gravel path outside Barrington's house, Sommer Chase, not far from the stables. A fine dew coated everything in silver, quieting the world. The smell of the sea drifted on the breeze, briny and cool.

He took a breath, slow and deliberate, and let it burn its way down into his chest. He wasn't sure what unsettled him more, that he'd survived or that he sometimes wished he hadn't.

Sommer-by-the-Sea. It looked just as he remembered. But he was not the same man.

The door behind him creaked, and Barrington's voice followed. "You'll catch a chill standing out here like that."

"I've been colder," Quinton said without turning.

Barrington joined him on the path and offered him a mug of coffee. "Kenworth tells me you didn't sleep."

"I'm not used to beds." He took a sip of the hot brew.

Barrington raised a brow. "Luxury clearly doesn't suit you."

Quinton shrugged. "Turns out, civilian linens are more cunning than French scouts."

Barrington didn't smile, though the corners of his mouth twitched. "You don't have to talk about it, you know."

"I know," Quinton said quietly. "But I probably should."

They walked in silence for a few minutes, the gravel crunching underfoot. Barrington didn't press. Quinton could feel the man's patience, honed like a blade over years of command. It should've grated, but instead, it settled like a cloak across his shoulders. The kind of silence only a friend could offer.

"The gravel's too tidy," Quinton muttered. "Makes a man uneasy."

Barrington arched a brow. "Kenworth considers it a matter of honor."

"That explains the perfectly aligned rosebushes. My prison was more forgiving." The smile on Quinton's face faded.

Quinton's coat was too thin, but he welcomed the bite of the morning air.

"I was scouting with a small unit of six men. We were to observe a suspected supply line east of Badajoz," he began, his voice low and steady. "But someone was waiting for us. They knew our route. Our timing. Everything."

Barrington's brow furrowed. "An informant?"

"I thought so. Still do. We walked right into it. Three men were slain where they stood. Two more died later from their wounds." He paused. "They took me alive. Bound, gagged, blindfolded. And then… nothing for days."

Barrington was silent.

"They didn't wear uniforms. They spoke French sometimes. English more often. One of them even had a London accent. They weren't regular soldiers. I never saw a flag or heard an official name."

"That's not a French prison," Barrington said.

"No. It was a house, secluded, rural, like something forgotten. The windows were shuttered, and the rooms were dim. I saw trees once. And a hedge maze, overgrown and still, as though no one had walked its paths in years."

"No guards. No interrogations. Just silence."

He didn't say the rest aloud. No sounds of life. No bells, no footsteps outside, not even birdsong. Only the creak of the floorboards and the sound of his own breath. The hedge maze he glimpsed once through a cracked shutter had looked overgrown, like something forgotten. Like him.

He could remember watching the leaves turn brown, wondering how many seasons had passed. The image still haunted him, tangled vines, narrowing paths, no clear exit, just like the feeling that hadn't yet left him.

"Why did they keep you alive?"

Quinton shook his head. "I've thought about that every day."

Barrington looked at him, his gaze sharp. "Did they question you?"

"Rarely. And when they did, they asked me odd questions. Not about military tactics. Nothing about troop movement. They asked about… people. Names. Locations."

Barrington swore under his breath and stiffened, his fingers tapping once against the mug. His eyes narrowed slightly, but he didn't speak. Not yet.

"I thought I was going mad," Quinton admitted. "But I held on to one thing."

Barrington waited.

"Mary-Ann."

The name settled between them like a dropped coin. Her name hadn't passed his lips in over three years. Just the sound of it again grounded him, as if memory and breath could become the same thing.

"I remembered the way she laughed when I told her the stars were brighter in Portugal. I remembered how she used to lean over my shoulder to correct my accounts." He paused, the memories catching in his throat. "I used to imagine her voice, what she'd say if she were there. I'd make up conversations just to hear something human. When it got really bad, I'd see her face in the dark, clear as candlelight. I think I clung to those thoughts because they were the only things that still felt real. I could forget who I was, what day it was," he turned to Barrington. "But never her."

He looked down at his coffee, fingers tightening slightly around the mug. "Even after the letters stopped coming, I kept reciting the ones I had in my head. Every word. Every line. I must have repeated them a thousand times."

Barrington took a deep breath and spoke quietly. "You're not the only one who couldn't forget. She waited longer than most would have," Barrington added. "Longer than some thought wise. She never stopped asking if we'd heard anything."

Barrington's voice softened. "She wrote letters to me, to my brother Edward, and to anyone she thought might know something, anyone who would listen. She traveled to London more than once to meet with officials at the War Office. When no one responded, she started copying every letter twice, sending one to the regiment and one to the Admiralty, just in case. She kept a map in her father's study with pins marking every place the brigade might've passed through. And every time she thought she was a nuisance, she apologized. But she never gave up."

Quinton stared at the mist curling along the fence posts. "I hoped," he said, at last, his voice low. "Even when the silence stretched on for months... I told myself she was still out there. Still fighting."

His hand tightened on the cooling mug. "There were nights when everything else slipped away except her. Her voice. Her letters, even if I never saw them. I made them up in my mind, imagined what she might say, just to hold on a little longer."

Quinton was quiet for a long moment. The coffee in his hand had gone cold. "I didn't know," he said finally. "I thought...when the letters stopped..."

"They didn't stop," Barrington said gently. "They weren't given to you."

He swallowed hard. "I didn't know what she was doing. But I knew who she was. That was enough to keep breathing."

Barrington nodded, then added, "She'd be glad to hear that."

Quinton looked back toward the house. "I need to tell her someday. That she saved me." He looked away, his jaw tightening slightly. "She's engaged to another man. I should be glad for her," he said, though the words tasted foreign. "But..."

"Wilkinson," Barrington said.

Quinton's mouth curved, not quite in a smile. "We weren't friends. Not truly. But I knew him."

Barrington said nothing.

Quinton took another sip of coffee. "He seemed very composed yesterday. Polite. Comfortable."

"He has a talent for blending in," Barrington said carefully.

A silence stretched between them, not uncomfortable but full of things left unsaid. Of names, of suspicions, of roads not yet taken.

"Do you trust him?" Quinton asked.

Barrington didn't answer immediately. "I don't distrust him. But I trust you, Quinton. And I know that look in your eyes."

Quinton nodded once. "I'm not done yet." His voice had steadied. It was low and certain, like a soldier choosing his ground. "Not with Mary-Ann. And not with what happened to me."

From the stables, the soft nicker of a horse broke the stillness.

"Kenworth will have breakfast ready," Barrington said. "Come in before you catch a chill."

Quinton didn't move right away. His gaze swept the misted fields, then lifted toward the cliffs where the sea met the sky like a dare.

Barrington paused at the door. "When you decide what comes next," he said quietly, "you won't be alone."

Quinton met his gaze. For the first time, he didn't feel like a ghost in borrowed clothes.

"I need to know why they let me live," he murmured.

He huffed a breath that wasn't quite a laugh. "Listen to me. Brooding on a cliffside. I sound like a gothic novel."

Barrington didn't reply. He only gave a dry snort, the kind that might mean agreement or amusement, and stepped inside.

Quinton glanced toward the house. He hadn't expected to find comfort in a valet with the sharp tongue of a field sergeant, but Kenworth had a way of making things feel... normal.

Kenworth was already waiting just beyond the threshold, a towel draped over one arm.

"The coffee's only marginally improved from yesterday," he said. "But there's a lemon tart left over. If you need a reason to go on living, my lord, that might suffice."

Quinton gave a soft laugh. It surprised even him.

"I heard the staff mention that they were reserved for brides threatening elopement?"

Kenworth opened the door wider. "Not these. Come in. Let the sea keep its chill."

Chapter Five

IT WAS TWO mornings later, beneath a sky the color of steel, the Seaton Shipping offices stood at the edge of the docks, a proud two-story brick building with green-shuttered windows and a wide slate roof that bore the salt and gull-marked wear of years by the sea. Beyond it, ships creaked in the morning tide, gulls circled overhead like sentinels. The scent of brine, tar, and freshly oiled wood hung thick in the air. Carts clattered over cobblestones as dockworkers laughed and shouted orders while some lifted crates and barrels.

Inside the office, Mary-Ann sat at her desk outside her father's office, the late morning light slanting through the high windows. Her sleeves were neatly pinned beneath linen protectors, a precaution she'd learned early when ink blotches ruined a favorite cuff. Even now, an ink stain smudged her wrist as she leafed through a shipment ledger. She stopped and turned to a previous page and studied the column of numbers. Her brow furrowed. Something wasn't right.

A shipment from Lisbon, three crates of dried fruit, and two filled with bolts of silk were marked as received and cleared. But she'd been down at the docks two days ago. Those crates never came off the *Winsome Tide*.

She turned the page back. Then forward again. The same tidy handwriting. The same signature initials.

"Father?" she called.

From the adjoining room, a gruff voice replied, "Yes?"

"This entry for the Lisbon cargo says it was received, but I never saw it come off the ship."

He appeared in the doorway, spectacles perched on the end of his nose. "Probably a delay in the offloading. You know that happens more often than you think."

She tapped the page. "But it's already marked as received and taxed."

He shrugged. Must have been sorted before you got there. These things are handled quickly when there's coin at stake."

Yet this time, something tugged at the edge of her thoughts. Not doubt, just a sense that the numbers didn't add up the way they always did.

She wasn't a child tallying figures for amusement. She knew the shipping routes, the taxes, and the weight of crates before they were even unlashed. And she trusted numbers. Numbers, at least, didn't misremember.

She stood and gathered the ledger and notes into a neat pile. Her fingers lingered on the ribbon, and her gaze drifted to the window where the mast tops swayed gently in the distance. The tide was coming in. She had always liked this time of day when the harbor stirred with motion, when the world felt full of purpose and quiet industry. But this morning, the tide's steady pull couldn't quite wash away the unease that clung to her.

And this time, she couldn't quite ignore it.

She had just begun to tie the stack with a ribbon when a familiar voice floated in from the doorway.

"Still buried in numbers, my love?"

Rodney stepped inside with a smile just shy of sincere and a small parcel wrapped in linen. "I brought you something from the bakery you like. Surely you can spare a moment for something sweet?"

Mary-Ann offered a polite smile. "That was thoughtful of you."

He moved closer, his gaze drifting over the desk, the papers, the ledgers as if none of it quite deserved to be there. "You've always had a curious fondness for figures. Most ladies I know would be content to plan their wedding."

She lifted her chin slightly. "I enjoy the work."

He set the parcel down on the edge of the desk. "Of course. But once we're married, you'll have more pleasant diversions than poring over ledgers." He turned toward the window, adding under his breath. "No more of this playing at bookkeeping."

Her hand stilled on the folio. She wasn't even sure why she opened it, except that she needed something familiar, something firm beneath her fingertips. Inside lay the arithmetic paper Mrs. Bainbridge had asked her to review, its clean sums now scored with her own careful red notes. Numbers. Order. Precision. Her world made sense here, and at this moment, it steadied her.

Rodney's voice, low and dismissive, still echoed in her ears. Not loud, but sharp enough to leave a mark.

Rodney turned back to her with another smile, expecting…what? Gratitude? Compliance?

She didn't return his smile.

A quiet twist curled in her stomach. Not because of what he said, but because of how he said it, offhanded, amused, the way one might speak of a child's whim. As if her work, her skills, were some idle indulgence he'd been tolerating. She wondered, not for the first time, how many other parts of her he planned to smooth away, reshape, or quietly set aside.

"I should finish up here," she said, not unkindly but without any warmth.

He held up his hands in a gesture of easy surrender. "Of course. I'll walk you home in an hour."

She gave a small nod but didn't look up, her eyes fixed instead on the student's paper.

The door closed gently behind him.

She had been grateful for his steadiness once. His calm presence was a boon in a world turned upside down. But today, he felt less like an anchor and more like a rope, gently tugging her away from the parts of herself she wasn't ready to relinquish.

Her gaze dropped again to the column of numbers. The Lisbon discrepancy tugged at her thoughts like a loose thread. She copied a few more notes, circled the missing crates, and added a short line beneath: Ask Father.

He glanced up from his desk when she approached him with a fond smile. "You're still chasing that Lisbon cargo?"

"It doesn't match the dock record," she said. "There are two crates not accounted for."

He shrugged. "It's likely still in storage or mislogged. You know how these things go."

"And Rodney?" she asked, keeping her tone casual. "He's a banker. Yet, you've had him reviewing the quarter reports?"

Her father leaned back slightly as if amused. "Rodney was asking a few questions. Said he wanted to understand the business better. He *is* a banker. Figures and ledgers come naturally to him. And he'll be part of the family soon enough. His interest is only normal."

Mary-Ann had nodded, but the answer didn't sit well. Rodney had never shown interest in the shipping operations before. And while her father had said it lightly, there had been something offhand about it, dismissive, as though it didn't matter.

But it did matter. Every crate, every tally, every conversation. And she would continue looking until it all made sense.

She didn't wait the full hour. She needed the air, the space. Needed to walk without someone watching her for signs of fatigue or a lapse in decorum.

She tucked the ledger beneath her arm and drew her shawl tighter against the rising wind, she left the office. The smell of brine and pitch hung in the air, the sound of the sea blending with the clatter of hooves and the low rumble of carts.

The long route along the docks was always livelier. Familiar. Here, she wasn't Miss Seaton, the betrothed young woman. She was simply Miss Mary-Ann, the shipowner's daughter, the girl who used to count crates for fun and ask too many questions about shipping manifests.

Crates thudded onto wheeled platforms. Ropes creaked above her as dockworkers coordinated the unloading of a tall brig moored near the seawall. Overhead, a large bale of cotton swung slowly on a pulley system, guided by shouted instructions and wary eyes.

A younger dockhand tipped his cap as she passed, and another called out, not unkindly, "Mind you don't start tallying our wages next, Miss Seaton."

She smiled faintly but said nothing. The familiarity of the banter was oddly comforting.

Sunlight reflected off the water in jagged shards, and the air was filled with the clang of chains and the deep thrum of a departing steamer's horn. A gull swooped overhead, scattering breadcrumbs from an upturned crate. She should have felt comforted by the familiar routine, the same crates, the same shouted orders, but the knot in her stomach refused to loosen.

She passed workers who had known her since she was a girl, men who had watched her grow into her father's shadow. One older man, Hamish, a trusted dock foreman with shoulders like stacked barrels and a permanent squint from years in the salt wind, caught her eye. He stepped away from a stack of crates, wiping his hands on a cloth as he approached. He didn't smile like he usually did. His gait was slower, his eyes flicking once toward the warehouse before settling on her.

"Miss Mary-Ann," he said with a respectful nod. "Been hoping I'd see you. There's something that's been bothering me."

She slowed her steps, brow furrowing. "Hamish, is something wrong?"

He glanced over his shoulder, not nervously, but with the wariness of someone careful with what could be overheard. "No, not wrong, exactly," he said. "Just been thinkin' on something. You've always had a sharp head for things, and you see more than most."

She tilted her head slightly. "What is it, Hamish?"

He hesitated, rubbing the back of his neck with a calloused

hand. "It's about him. He's not—"

A sharp shout cut through the air. "Move, miss!"

Hamish's arm shot out, pushing her aside. She stumbled back, the ledger pressed against her chest. Above them, ropes snapped with a sickening twang. A block and tackle, iron and wood, spun free from the hoist and plummeted to the dock.

It struck Hamish with a sound that was more felt than heard.

Time stuttered. The air rushed from her lungs, but her body moved before her mind caught up. She was calling for help, even as everything inside her screamed to undo what had just happened.

Mary-Ann's scream pierced the air as Hamish dropped to the planks. The ledger slipped from her hands, scattering pages in the wind. Dockworkers shouted, some running, others frozen in place. But she moved. She was at Hamish's side in seconds, falling to her knees. Blood was already pooling beneath him.

"Fetch Dr. Manning!" she cried. "Quickly!" She glanced overhead. "And get this rigging checked. Now!"

She gave Hamish her full attention, but she knew. From the unnatural stillness. From the way the breath never came.

Hamish's fingers twitched. He struggled to breathe. "Ink..." he whispered.

Her head dipped close, tears already falling.

"On your nose," he murmured, his voice no more than a memory. "Always had ink on your nose, little miss..." His lips lifted, barely. And then he stilled.

Hands were already moving, boots pounding across the dock. She scanned the pulley line overhead, and her stomach turned. She crouched beside the rigging, reaching out with a steady hand to inspect the frayed end. It hadn't come loose. She'd seen ropes wear down before. The fibers unraveled in weather and time, but this break was too abrupt, too clean. Whoever had done this hadn't meant to miss. The question was, had they meant to kill Hamish... or someone else? She rose slowly, her heart pounding.

Someone stood beside her, Jonas, a younger dockhand with

wide eyes and trembling hands. He held out the ledger with the pages reassembled as best he could, the ribbon slightly torn but still wrapped tight. "Miss Mary-Ann... I think this is yours."

She took it with a numb nod, brushing grit from the cover.

Something inside her had shifted. Not just grief. Resolve. Someone had turned her docks into a hunting ground, and she would not let them take another soul. A dark smear marred one corner, blood or grease, she couldn't say. She clutched it to her chest again, fingers tight. Not just to protect it. But to steady herself.

One of the crew covered Hamish with a sailcloth. The world hadn't stopped moving. But inside her, something had gone very, very still.

The cries and footfalls faded around her, distant echoes in a world that had tilted on its axis. She brushed her skirts, her hands trembling, before she forced them still. There was no room for panic now. Grief would come later. For now, there was only action. She turned to a group of stunned dockworkers nearby.

"Check every hoist line on this dock," she ordered. "Start at the rigging and work your way down. If anything appears to be wrong, frayed, in tension, or with knots, report it to the office immediately."

Her voice did not waver, and for a heartbeat, no one moved. Three men nodded and took off at a run. And beneath it, something colder still. She had a growing certainty that this was no accident.

Chapter Six

THAT SAME AFTERNOON, the wind off the sea was sharper, sweeping through the docks and carrying with it the scent of salt and smoke. Mary-Ann sat stiffly in her father's carriage, her hands clenched in her lap, her folio with the rumpled pages of the ledger tucked inside. The seat beneath her felt too fine, the carriage too quiet. Her mind wandered to Hamish, not just the man who died but the man she'd known since childhood.

Once, he let her borrow his cap and shout orders to invisible sailors. The crew played along, saluting with mock-serious expressions as Hamish stood behind her, arms crossed, pretending to take notes. She hadn't thought of that moment in years. But now, it shimmered like a coin on the sea floor. He'd winked when she memorized routes faster than the shipping master. And now… now he was gone, taken not by time or illness but by something darker. Her father had barely looked at the spot where it happened.

Across from her, her father stared straight ahead, silent save for the occasional sigh. He hadn't spoken much since the accident. Not beyond insisting she leave the scene and return home.

"It was an accident, Mary-Ann," he said finally, as if rehearsing it aloud might make it true. "Rigging can fail if it's not properly maintained. Hamish should have had it checked twice, if not three times."

She turned her face to the window. She'd known Hamish

since she was a girl, climbing crates and pretending to command ships. He'd let her balance on the beams of the empty docks, always with a steady hand nearby, always patient. And now his last breath had been spent trying to warn her. About what? Or… about whom? "He was coming to tell me something."

Her father didn't reply.

"He said, 'He's not—' and then he was gone." Her voice cracked. "You didn't see his face. He looked afraid."

It wasn't only what her father said. It was what he refused to see. His eyes never met hers. As if looking too long might reveal something he didn't want to acknowledge. About Hamish. About her. About himself.

"A man died, Mary-Ann," her father said, more firmly now. "Let that be enough. It's done."

She wanted to scream at him, not in grief, but in frustration. She wanted to shake him, to demand he take off his blinders and see what she had seen. But she said nothing. What was the use? Her father had built his world on the certainties of shipping routes, profit margins, and well-paid loyalties. Anything that threatened that order, he dismissed as an inconvenience or imagination. And she was his daughter, sharp, yes, but still a woman. Still, someone to be comforted and guided, not believed.

When they reached the house, the footman helped her down, and she entered without waiting for anyone. Her shoes clicked briskly along the marble foyer until she reached the study. She closed the door behind her.

There, in the hush of oil-polished wood and shelves of account books, she let the tension melt just enough to lower herself into the chair. She laid the ledger on the desk in front of her. For a moment, she didn't move. The silence in the study wasn't peaceful. It felt expectant, coiled like something waiting to spring. She exhaled, trying to gather her thoughts, but they skittered like loose pages in a breeze.

The stillness felt too thick, too intentional, as if the room itself were waiting for her to make a mistake. She ran her fingers along the edge of the ledger. Her hand trembled, not from grief but from the sharp edge of suspicion cutting deeper than she was prepared to admit. She stared at it. The cracked leather cover, the scent of ink and starch and salt from the docks. It all felt suddenly sinister. What had once been numbers and routine now looked like a cipher. A mask. A trail she hadn't known she was following.

A soft knock came at the door. Before she could answer, it opened.

"Mary-Ann?" Wilkinson.

He entered with careful steps, like someone entering a chapel. "I came as soon as I heard. My God, are you all right?"

She nodded. "I'm fine."

"That must've been dreadful," he said, kneeling beside her chair. He reached for her hand.

She didn't pull away. But she didn't return the pressure, either. Her hand rested in his like something forgotten.

"You don't have to talk about it," he said gently. "Just say the word, and I'll see to it that your father doesn't trouble you with these ledgers again."

Her gaze sharpened. "I'm not fragile, Rodney."

He blinked. "Of course not. Forgive me. I only meant that no one would find fault if you needed to rest."

Mary-Ann said nothing. But the quiet between them thickened. He hadn't asked what she'd seen, hadn't even wondered aloud if the accident had truly been one. It was all smoothed-over concern, carefully chosen words. And now, he wanted to strip away the one thing that gave her a sense of control. The ledgers. Her work. Her instincts.

He stood slowly. Mary-Ann watched him without rising, her eyes sharp despite the ache behind them. He didn't glance at the ledger again, nor did he ask what she was working on. Only smoothed his sleeve and gave her that same distant, polished smile.

"I'll give you some time. We'll speak later."

She nodded again, but only after he'd turned away. When she

heard his footsteps fade down the hall, she let her shoulders sag. His presence lingered like perfume that had turned sour. He had always been like this, hadn't he? Always saying the right thing and offering sympathy in perfectly measured doses. But there was never a question, never a curiosity that reached beyond the surface. She hadn't seen it clearly before. But now, after today, it felt glaring. She hadn't imagined that chill beneath the warmth. She simply hadn't wanted to name it. So careful. So controlled. So... empty. Quinton wouldn't have offered comfort before understanding the wound. He would have asked. Pressed. Refused to look away.

A short time later, another knock sounded. This time, it was Hollis with two notes on a silver tray.

The first was penned in Mrs. Bainbridge's careful script:

My dear, I've just heard. If you'd like company, I'd be honored to sit with you for a while. If not, know that I am near. You need not carry this alone.

With affection, Honoria Bainbridge

The second was in a more masculine hand, the paper crisp and the dark ink, a note from Barrington's household.

Miss Seaton, Lord Rockingham, asked me to convey his concern. Should you require anything, please know you have only to ask.

Respectfully, Preston Kenworth

Her throat tightened. Neither note asked her to be anything but herself. Not useful. Not composed. Just... cared for. It steadied her more than tea or silence ever had. She stared at the notes for a long time, then pressed them gently between the pages of the ledger before closing it.

She hadn't imagined it. Quinton would ask. And when she was ready, she would answer.

She opened her folio and leafed through the ledger pages

again, this time more slowly. She examined the notes in the margins, tally marks, and names.

She'd been trained to read numbers the way others read maps or stories. Subtle shifts meant more than missing crates. They revealed intent. A delayed shipment. An added tax line. Things no one else would question, but she could feel the patterns. Like the sea pulling back before a wave. The Lisbon cargo still stood out. But now something else did too. Her breath caught. One discrepancy might be a mistake. Two was a pattern. Her heart began to race, not with fear this time, but with clarity. She hadn't imagined the unease. There was something hiding beneath the ink.

The Carrabelle. Two crates of ink and five of spices, at least, that's what the official ledger claimed. But the dock report she'd filed that day listed only three crates. She'd seen them offloaded herself.

She rose, moving to the small cabinet where she kept personal records, logs she maintained independently. She'd done so since she was sixteen, for practice, her father said.

There it was. *The Carrabelle's* arrival. The notation in her hand: Three crates received. Discrepancy noted. Thomas unaware.

She stared at it.

Hamish's voice echoed in her mind. *He's not—*

She didn't know who he referred to. But the words haunted her. She turned them over in her mind like a riddle, unfinished and incomplete. She could almost feel Hamish's urgency in those last seconds. That wasn't a man casually warning a friend. That was someone terrified of being too late.

Someone had made those shipments disappear from the records. And someone else wanted her to stop looking. She closed the cabinet and locked it. And if no one else intended to find the truth, she would.

She moved to the window, the ledger still in hand. Outside, the sea shifted under slate-grey clouds, the tide rising. Mary-Ann touched the window's edge, cool beneath her fingers, and pictured Hamish's weathered face, the way he always seemed to know the wind before it turned. He'd trusted her once. Believed in her instincts. And now, whether anyone else did or not, she would believe in them too. She didn't know where the answers lay, only that they wouldn't come from her father or from the man who thought her too delicate to keep books. If there was a traitor, she would name him. Not for glory. Not for vengeance. For Hamish, who had tried to warn her.

The sky beyond the glass darkened at the edges, but her thoughts were sharp, bright as a lantern. The tide was rising. So was she. If no one else would bring this to light, she would. Let the wind howl and the sea rage. She would not look away.

Chapter Seven

THE NEXT MORNING began with the scent of burnt sugar wafting down the corridor of Sommer Chase. Quinton paused on the landing, one brow raised. It wasn't an unpleasant scent, exactly, but it did not bode well. From below came the muffled sound of arguing or possibly strategizing. Or both.

He descended the staircase cautiously, hand skimming the polished banister, until he stepped into the drawing room and stopped short.

Three footmen stood like soldiers, each with a plate of half-eaten cake, one pale with shock, one chewing slowly as if unsure whether to swallow, and one grimacing as though betrayed. A young maid was dusting powdered sugar off the edge of the rug. In the center of the chaos stood Kenworth, holding a fork like a weapon. One of the cakes, lavender sponge with sugared violets, still trembled slightly on a silver tray as if it were offended.

"Tell me again," Kenworth said dryly to the stout baker before him, "why the almond cake needs to taste like syrup of squills."

The baker sputtered. "It's traditional."

"So was bloodletting," Kenworth mumbled.

Barrington appeared in the doorway, took one look at the room, and muttered, "I should've taken Honoria to Greta Green."

"You'd have spared your household," Quinton offered mildly.

"I'd have spared myself." Barrington shook his head as he

surveyed the room.

Kenworth inclined his head toward Barrington. "My lord, the third cake is tolerable. The second was aggressively floral. The first... we will not speak of the first."

"I left orders for no tastings until this afternoon," Barrington muttered. "Honoria said nothing of a tasting this morning."

"Mrs. Bainbridge," Kenworth said, "sent the cakes. Along with a note that reads, and I quote, 'A morning treat!'"

Quinton bit back a smile. There was something comforting in the absurdity. After weeks of closed doors and cautious stares, this...this ridiculous display of confectionery warfare felt like a breath of fresh air and the closest thing to normal he'd known. Since Barrington had pulled him from the remains of that nameless outpost in Spain, little had felt real. But this? This was human and somewhat hilarious.

Barrington blew out a breath, the kind only a man in love, and trapped by buttercream, might release. "Where's Simms? This seems like a punishment he deserves."

"In France," Kenworth replied. "Where cake is properly made."

"Gentlemen." Barrington gestured to the door. He turned to Kenworth. "Tell Mrs. Bainbridge I'm indisposed and unable to taste cakes at the moment." He ran his hand through his hair and muttered. "I'll invent a diplomatic emergency."

The footmen, still holding their plates like sacrificial offerings, exchanged glances. One, perhaps emboldened by Barrington's evident suffering, dared to take another bite. His expression instantly crumbled into regret. "Still dreadful," he muttered.

Kenworth merely set his fork down with finality. "My lord, if I may, this particular confection should be classified as a weapon rather than a dessert."

One of the footmen, caught mid-chew, coughed politely into his napkin, his eyes watering. Kenworth delicately lifted a ruined doily from beneath the offending slice and examined it as if it held clues to sabotage. "My lord," Kenworth said, setting the doily back in place with finality, "this particular confection may be better suited to patching hulls than serving at a wedding breakfast."

Barrington leaned in, squinting at the cake like a general surveying a failed campaign. "The cherries look suspect."

"Those are raspberries, my lord," the baker said.

"Precisely." Barrington smiled at him.

The baker, clearly offended, threw up his hands. "Perhaps His Lordship's palate is simply unsuited for the finer things."

Barrington exhaled. "If the finer things taste like disappointment, then perhaps. I believe we've had quite enough cake for one morning. Please have it taken away.

Kenworth gave a short bow. "I shall inform Mrs. Bainbridge that your affections have been temporarily compromised by cake." He added, with the faintest hint of amusement, "She also wrote, 'Tell Barrington he must select a cake by Monday, or I shall elope with the lemon tart.'"

"Well, that's a tart ultimatum." Barrington tried not to laugh.

"Come, Barrington," Quinton said. "You certainly don't want to sour her plans."

There was a ripple of restrained amusement among the footmen. Even the housemaid allowed the corners of her mouth to twitch as she swept the powdered sugar into her tin.

Kenworth gave a single approving nod as if pleased to see Quinton engaging in the room's absurdity.

Barrington glanced between them, resigned. "Excellent. I shall become the subject of household comedy. Again."

As the staff left the room, Quinton lingered with his hands in his pockets, staring at the last unfortunate remnants of cake scattered across plates and trays. The laughter had settled, but its warmth still echoed.

How long had it been since he'd been part of something so… ordinary? Not standing at attention. Not calculating the number of rations left in a camp. Not scanning for threats.

Just men arguing over sponge cake. He watched how one of

the footmen silently slid the tray away without a word, how the maid swept sugar into neat spirals instead of rushing. It wasn't just an order. It was affection built into the routine. These weren't the hurried, fearful movements of servants he'd seen in other households. Here, everything moved with ease and affection. It felt like family. It's strange how much you can learn from the way people handle crumbs.

His fingers curled slightly. The strangest things made a man feel human again. And the strangest things made him remember how much of himself had been missing.

As the room emptied, Kenworth lingered, gathering the utensils with brisk efficiency. He paused only once beside Quinton, his voice low. "It's good to have the house noisy again."

Quinton met his eyes, surprised by the comment. For a man who had grown used to being a shadow in other people's periphery, the quiet acknowledgment settled deeper than expected.

"Even if it comes with cake casualties," Kenworth added.

Quinton's lips curved. "I can agree with you."

"You're smiling," Barrington noted.

"Am I?" That only made him smile more.

"Like a man who remembers what normal feels like." Barrington ran his finger through the dusted sugar on the table.

Quinton's smile eased, though not completely. "It's strange," he said quietly. "The things that make you feel human again. Even bad cake and worse puns."

He glanced around the room, taking in the remnants of the absurd spectacle, the lopsided cake slices, the footman still licking a finger behind the curtain, the smell of lavender sponge lingering like perfume. For the first time in years, he wasn't surrounded by shadows or silence. It was a household filled with ordinary trials and affection beneath the surface. It didn't feel like a battlefield. It felt like something worth returning to.

He remembered one night in Portugal, eating scorched oats from a blackened pot beside a man who didn't live to see morning. That had been normal once. Boots soaked, smoke in the air, laughter cutting through fear. This was different. This was warmth without warning, peace that didn't need explanation. It was foreign, and it was welcome.

Barrington wiped the sugar from his hand on a linen, crossed the room, and poured two short glasses of brandy. "You know," he said, "you used to tell the worst jokes in camp. Men groaned louder than they did at musket fire."

"Some things haven't changed." Quinton tried not to smile.

Barrington's smile was faint. "But some things have. I'm glad you're back, Quinton. You were always meant to return." As he moved, Kenworth stepped back in silently and placed a small, sealed envelope on the mantel. Quinton barely had to glance at it to recognize the crest, an old contact of Edward Oakdene's, Barrington's older brother.

"Have you reached out to Mary-Ann?"

Quinton turned at Barrington's question and nodded slowly. "After I heard about Hamish, I sent her a note through Kenworth. I asked him to tell her I was available if she needed anything."

Barrington lifted his glass. "A fair offering."

"She replied," Quinton added, almost carefully. "Through Mrs. Bainbridge. Just a few words to express her gratitude for the message, and she hoped I was recovering well. Mrs. Bainbridge passed along her note."

Barrington met his eyes. "She didn't have to respond at all."

"No," Quinton said. "But she did."

He hadn't realized how much he needed to hear from her until Mrs. Bainbridge shared Mary-Ann's words, written in her hand.

The handwriting was still precise, still hers. She'd used his title, but not coldly. And at the end, there had been one phrase, "Take care, always," a phrase she whispered once on a cliffside before he left for Spain.

He looked down into his glass, then up at the mantel. "It's not much. But it's something. A thread, maybe. And after everything… It's enough." For now, he added silently.

There was a pause. The fire snapped softly behind them.

"She was with Hamish when the accident happened," Quinton added. "Kenworth heard the story from the staff. Apparently, she acted fast. Had someone go after Dr. Manning and had the men check all the rigging. But the rigging—"

"I know," Barrington said. "Word travels fast in port towns. And quietly, if you know how to listen."

Quinton turned the glass in his hand. "The break in the rope was too clean. Not weathered or frayed. It doesn't feel like a coincidence."

"It doesn't," Barrington agreed. "But we don't name shadows until we see what casts them. We wait."

"No," Quinton added. "We start looking."

Barrington studied him for a long moment. "You're not just staying for her."

Quinton met Barrington's steady gaze. "No," Quinton said. "But she's the reason I crossed oceans to return. Whatever this is, whatever's happening, I'm not sitting on the sidelines."

Barrington reached for his glass. "Good. Because I've already begun asking questions."

Quinton glanced at the message on the mantel. He didn't reach for it yet. The seal bore the familiar crest of an old Brigade contact. One Edward had once trusted with secrets too dangerous for ink. The paper was cool, untouched, but it hummed with tension. A name, a time, a piece of truth someone had gone to great lengths to bury. Any of these could be inside.

He wasn't sure what would be worse: finding answers or uncovering more questions. The kind that changed the shape of loyalties. And of lives.

He hadn't told anyone, not even Barrington, what he'd promised himself that last night in Spain.

Outside, the bells of a passing carriage jingled cheerfully. Inside, beneath the chandelier that still bore a faint dusting of sugar like the aftermath of some genteel skirmish, two former soldiers raised a quiet toast.

Quinton gestured toward the letter. "It reminds me of a phrase Edward once used. *'A clean seal hides the dirtiest truths.'* And if Edward had sent this... it isn't a correspondence. It's a summons. The kind we can't ignore."

Neither knew what the letter held, but whatever it was, it meant their reprieve was at an end. Barrington refreshed their glasses.

"To battles old and new." Barrington raised his glass.

Quinton clinked his glass gently against Barrington's. This time, he didn't drink to the past. He drank to the future, to the questions still waiting, to the woman he could never forget, and to the vow he'd made beneath Spanish skies: that he would return, offer his heart, and accept whatever choice she made.

He'd made it silently, staring up at a ceiling of stars in a broken camp. If he lived, he would return. If she still loved him, he would ask her to marry him. Not out of duty. Out of love.

Chapter Eight

THE MOON WAS high without a cloud in the sky. The stars twinkled and glowed. The house had long since gone quiet, the kind of hush that settled deep into the beams and brick after the last footman had gone to bed and the coals on the hearth had begun to dim. Mary-Ann sat alone in her father's study. The candle burned low, casting shadows across the polished desk.

Her fingers were smudged with ink again. The ledgers, her father's official shipping records, and her own private notes were spread in front of her. Her private notes were intended to serve as a learning tool. But lately, it had become something else.

Five crates were listed in one book. Three were reported at the docks.

That had to be wrong. She turned back a page, checked the supplier's initials, then the weight. Identical. She leafed forward. A different arrival port, a different date, but the same inventory code. Her pulse ticked up.

She leaned back in her chair and glanced at the upper shelf. Hamish's old ledger was still there, tucked beside the annual indexes…She remembered how he used to steady the scale with one thick hand while she read the figures aloud, nodding approvingly when she spotted a discrepancy before he did. Hamish had trusted her with more than numbers. He had given her quiet encouragement, a belief that she saw clearly, perhaps more clearly than some wished her to. She could still hear his voice sometimes, low and gruff but always patient when he taught her how to read manifests or warned her never to trust a cargo count until she'd verified it herself. Hamish had been more than a dock manager. He had been a quiet sort of guardian, a man who saw more than he ever said. His absence still echoed in the quiet places of the house. She missed him more than she dared to admit.

"You'd know what to make of this," she whispered. "You always did."

She didn't wait for the silence to answer. Instead, she returned to the desk and pulled another volume toward her. There had to be more. A thread. A slip. Something.

The candle sputtered, casting the shadow of her profile across the page. Her head ached from squinting, and her shoulders were stiff, but still, she pushed on. If Hamish had died trying to tell her something, she owed it to him to listen to what the numbers told her. And she couldn't shake the feeling that the truth was somewhere in these pages, buried under ink and polite deception.

She stared at the names again, *Carrabelle, Redwake, Winsome Tide*. They had appeared before. She was certain of it. She crossed to the shelves, scanning the spines until her hand hovered over an older ledger. This old ledger was Hamish's first year managing independent dock operations. If he had ever flagged problems with these ships, it would be there.

At last, she turned toward the shelf. The old ledger, Hamish's, waited like a quiet witness She reached for the thick volume on the upper shelf behind the desk. She slid it free and set it on the desk.

Carefully, she opened the cover. The pages crackled softly, brittle with age. She leafed through the first half of the book, scanning the tidy rows of cargo logs written in Hamish's hand, which was characteristically heavy and loopy. He used to cram notes into the margins of manifests with quick judgments about crews or cargo. She got to the back of the book and found newer entries. This ink was darker, and the writing was definitely not Hamish's. This handwriting was almost impatient. The pages were neat. Too neat. A prickle ran up her spine. She glanced over her shoulder. Nothing moved, there was no sound but the low tick of the mantel clock. Still, the air felt heavier somehow, charged. Her fingers hesitated on the page. It wasn't just the neatness. It was the sense that whoever wrote this didn't care to explain themselves. This wasn't a record. It was a private reckoning.

No. This wasn't Hamish's at all. Someone else had written this, someone who didn't expect other eyes to read it.

As she was about to close the old ledger, her fingers brushed something lodged between the binding and the cover. She turned the cover back and caught the edge of a slim, cloth-bound booklet, its spine barely visible against the seam. Carefully, she eased it free and turned it over in her hands. There was no title. The cloth cover was worn, plain, and soft from use. Whoever it belonged to hadn't wanted it labeled. Or found.

The paper inside was rough and of low quality, with ink bleeding slightly along the grain. Someone had written these notes quickly or carelessly.

Mary-Ann traced a finger down the margin. Symbols, names, ship titles. The entries weren't organized like her father's books. These were coded. Intimate. And familiar, somehow. She paged ahead and caught a distinctive curl in the capital "H" and the flourish on a descending "G." Her breath caught. She leafed back to the newer entries at the end of the old ledger and found the same impatient strokes. Whoever had used the back pages had written this as well. She returned to the booklet and read on.

Some of the names she recognized: The *Carrabelle*. The *Red-wake*. And again, the *Winsome Tide*. They were all ships connected to discrepancies.

She sat back, her heart thudding. This wasn't a second copy of official records. This was something else entirely.

These weren't official errors. These were patterns. The same ships, again and again. And someone, whoever wrote this, had been tracking them. Quietly. Illegally. Which meant they already knew what she suspected. That the crates were being diverted long before the ship left the dock.

And Hamish had kept this book hidden. Not destroyed. Not discarded. Hidden. He'd known it was dangerous, but also that someone might need it.

Her mind drifted to her father. He was methodical, principled, and always precise with numbers and names. He trusted his managers to handle the day-to-day work of the docks, but he reviewed the ledgers himself every quarter. If he had seen this, would he have dismissed it? Or had someone made sure he never laid eyes on it at all? She hated the creeping doubt that whispered through her. When she was a girl, she'd sit cross-legged on the rug while he worked, asking endless questions about tariffs and tonnage, all of which he answered with patient delight. He was proud of his precision, of knowing exactly where every coin had come from, and every crate was bound. To question that now felt like pulling at the foundation stones of her childhood. And yet, here she was, ledger open, truth unraveling.

She didn't want to believe her father had been careless or, worse, manipulated. But the deeper she looked, the more difficult it became to convince herself that it was all a coincidence. She used to believe her father knew everything that happened beneath the Seaton banner. But now, that belief felt less like certainty and more like a bedtime story. The kind told to keep children safe from the dark.

Her fingers tightened on the pages. Who had written this? And why was it hidden?

Mary-Ann rose and crossed to the window, pulling the heavy curtain aside just enough to see the quiet street beyond.

The street lay still, steeped in that half-moon silver that turned every edge soft and strange. Her breath fogged the glass as she leaned closer. Throughout her life, she had always felt safe in this house and this town. But now it felt like something had shifted beneath her feet, as though nothing was quite what it seemed anymore. For the first time, the darkness outside seemed to be watching her. No one lingered. The town was asleep. But that didn't mean she was alone.

She returned to the desk and sat slowly, turning another page. In her younger years, she'd found comfort in the quiet of the house at night, curling up by the library hearth with a book. But tonight, the hush felt hollow, stretched too thin. The shadows seemed longer than they should, and the tick of the clock struck harder. There were strange symbols next to some of the entries, triangles, dots, and slashes. Some cargo items were circled, others underlined. Whoever had written it had their own system, and it made her skin prickle to know she was looking at something not meant for her eyes.

A strange tightness gathered at the base of her throat. The symbols blurred for a moment as her eyes scanned too quickly, desperate to make sense of it all. A single slash beside the name Winsome Tide caught her attention. What did it mean? She didn't know, but her stomach turned as if her body understood before her mind could catch up. She pressed her palm flat against the desk to steady herself, then stiffened at a faint sound in the corridor. Her mouth went dry. Every sound sharpened, the tick of the clock, the rush in her ears. She didn't breathe. The knob turned again, and she prepared to lie, or flee, or—She held her breath, straining to hear more. The sound came again, slow, deliberate, like a footstep just beyond the door. Her heart pounded against her ribs. She reached instinctively for the booklet, sliding it closed, her mind racing with excuses, another creak, and then the doorknob turned.

Mary-Ann froze.

She closed the booklet quickly and slid it into her own writing folio. Then she reached for the official ledger and opened it wide, keeping her expression neutral just as the door to the study eased open.

It was Mrs. Aldridge, the housekeeper, her hair wrapped, her shawl clutched around her shoulders. "You'll work yourself to parchment at this rate," she murmured, not unkindly. "One of these nights, I'll find you tucked between the ledger pages like a cat on the hearth. Forgive me, miss," she whispered, "I heard someone moving and thought…"

"I couldn't sleep," Mary-Ann said softly. "Just some bookkeeping."

Mrs. Aldridge gave her a knowing look but didn't press. "Would you like tea?"

"No, thank you. I won't be long."

"Very well. Don't sit up too late, miss."

The housekeeper left, closing the door behind her.

Mary-Ann exhaled slowly and opened the folio just a crack to confirm the cloth-bound ledger was still tucked inside. She looked down at her hands, the ink staining her fingertips, the paper smudged where she had gripped it too tightly. Her heart still raced. She wasn't simply playing with books and numbers anymore. This was real. This was dangerous.

She pushed the ledgers into neat stacks, returned the larger one to its place, and tucked her writing folio under her arm. She would find the truth, page by page, if she had to. As she blew out the candle, the room sank into darkness once more, but her mind was alight.

She thought of Quinton, her Quint, how he had looked standing in the doorway, thinner than he should be, quieter than he once was, but unbroken. She could almost hear his voice, playful and cynical. *'You never did leave a puzzle unsolved, Mary-Ann.'*

She remembered how he used to stride through a room with barely contained energy, the glint in his eyes when he bested her at chess or pretended not to, just to hear her crow with triumph. There had been something in his eyes when he looked at her, something more than surprise or relief.

Despite everything, she still cared. And she ought not to. She had promised herself to another. Rodney, steady and proper, who spoke of plans and investments as if love were a ledger to be balanced. But Quinton had never been tidy like that. He had been wind and flame, impossible to chart. And somehow, he still was.

Even though she had tried to let go, the sight of him had stirred something too lasting to be buried. He had returned, not knowing what he would find, and he had stood there anyway. If he could face that, then she could face this. She would follow the threads wherever they led. She had played the obedient daughter long enough, smiled through compromises and polite silences. But this? This was hers to uncover. If no one else would ask the questions, then she would.

Whatever this book meant, someone had gone to great lengths to keep it hidden. That made it dangerous. And now, it was hers.

Chapter Nine

T HE FOLLOWING MORNING broke under grey skies. Mary-Ann awoke with the uneasy awareness that she hadn't truly slept. The morning light pressed against the curtains, cool and flat. Her head ached, not from illness but from too many thoughts packed too tightly into too few hours of rest.

She dressed quietly and glanced at her locked wardrobe, where she had hidden the cloth-bound ledger, tucked into the back beneath a folded shawl. She didn't know yet what the ledger meant or why it had been hidden in the first place, but that fact alone told her it was worth protecting. If someone had gone to the trouble of concealing it, then she needed to keep it safe until she understood why. She tested the lock twice before stepping away.

Downstairs, the house stirred to life. Mrs. Aldridge had already ordered tea and toast in the breakfast room, and the air smelled faintly of jam and firewood. It should have felt like any other morning. But it didn't.

Her father had already left for the docks. She was grateful. She needed time to think.

She took her tea standing at the window, the porcelain warm in her hand, though she barely tasted it. Her thoughts kept circling around the ships named in the hidden book, *Carrabelle, Redwake, Winsome Tide,* and the strange symbols etched beside the entries.

She considered asking her father about the ships directly, but every instinct warned her against it. She didn't have enough information. Not yet. If she raised the alarm without cause, she risked more than embarrassment. She could lose his confidence in her, and she had worked far too hard for that.

There was someone else she wanted to speak to. Someone who would listen, not dismiss her. The name came before she could stop it, Quinton. She exhaled softly, the thought far too tempting. Too dangerous.

She sipped her tea instead.

A knock at the door interrupted her musing.

"Miss Mary-Ann." Mrs. Aldridge stepped in with a note card in her hand. "Mr. Wilkinson is here."

Mary-Ann set the teacup down with care. "Show him in."

Rodney entered moments later, gloved and smiling, impeccably dressed as always. "You're up early," he said. I was passing by and thought I'd bring you these.

He held out a bouquet of blush-pink roses, delicate and full. The scent reached her first, heady and sweet, the kind that lingered. His gloved hand brushed against hers as he handed them to her, the leather cool and too smooth, too polished.

"They're lovely," Mary-Ann said, accepting them with a polite smile.

He studied her face. "You look tired. I hope you haven't been unwell?

"Only restless," she said lightly. "A great many things are on my mind."

"That's understandable. The wedding, the household, and all the arrangements. It's a great deal."

She nodded.

"It won't always be such a burden," he added. "You've carried more than your share. Balancing books and responsibilities when you ought to be enjoying the season."

He reached for her hand, holding it lightly between his gloved fingers. "When we're married, I'd like you to have that chance."

That chance. It was thoughtful. Generous. But it felt like a door softly closing.

Of course, life would change. That was what marriage meant, sharing everything. But for the first time, she wasn't certain whether that sharing meant becoming more…or becoming less.

She withdrew her hand gently and masked her unease with a sip of tea.

She stiffened slightly, hoping it wasn't visible. She had never considered her responsibilities a burden, not when they gave her purpose, not when they rooted her to the life she understood.

"I don't find it a burden."

He chuckled. "You've always been fond of your books and figures. But you'll see. Once we're settled, you won't need to worry over ledgers."

Her gaze sharpened, but she said nothing.

Rodney reached for her hand. "I worry for you, Mary-Ann. You're too fine to be tucked away behind numbers."

She eased her hand back gently. "And yet the numbers are how my father built this house. How he built everything we have."

He faltered, just a flicker. "Of course. I didn't mean—only that I want you to have a life of comfort and freedom from worry.

A life without purpose, a life she had fought hard for.

Mary-Ann nodded slowly. "That's kind of you."

There was a silence that stretched between them. Rodney broke it with a gentler tone.

"You know, when we're married, I'd like to take you to the coast. Somewhere quiet. Just the two of us. No schedules. No accounts."

For a moment, the idea didn't seem terrible. She imagined wind on her cheeks, salt in the air, a day without figures or decisions pressing at her. His voice was gentle now, touched by something almost wistful.

She glanced at him. He looked…hopeful. Maybe even sincere.

It was a lovely thought. A simple kind of happiness. But somehow it didn't feel like hers.

She smiled politely. "That sounds… peaceful."

He kissed her knuckles and glanced toward the hallway. "I mustn't stay long. I only wanted to see you."

His gaze lingered too long not quite on her, but past her, toward the writing folio on the side table, the one she used for everyday notes. She resisted the urge to move it, to shield it. Instead, she smiled and said nothing, even as something in her chest went very still.

"You've always been clever that way."

She rose politely as Mr. Hollis appeared to see him out. Rodney paused in the entryway before stepping outside.

"You know," he said, adjusting his collar, "you always look too deeply, my dear. Not everything in the world needs to be solved."

She held his gaze, her face unreadable. "Doesn't it?"

He smiled faintly. "Sometimes a thing is just what it seems. And sometimes it isn't worth the trouble to find out which."

He bowed and left.

Mary-Ann closed the door slowly and turned the lock with deliberate care.

The scent of roses clung to the air, soft and floral, but it lingered too long, too insistently, like something meant to distract. She stood motionless, listening to the silence that followed in Wilkinson's wake.

FOR SO LONG, his charm had made sense. He had been the practical choice, steady, well-spoken, admired in town. He had been thoughtful, always knowing what to say. Even when he hadn't stirred her the way Quinton once had, she had told herself love could grow where kindness lived.

And maybe it still could.

She crossed slowly to the window and parted the curtain with one hand to peer out into the street. Rodney had always spoken gently. Always with care. For a time, she had believed that was enough.

Perhaps it still could be.

But Quinton had never needed polished words. His presence alone had carried meaning.

Now, standing at the window, she saw the difference clearly for the first time.

How had she not noticed it before?

Was this just nerves? The natural unease before a marriage? Or had something deeper shifted without her realizing it?

Very well, Mary-Ann. That's enough. This isn't the time to be chasing ghosts or second-guessing what has already been decided.

The feeling would pass. It had to.

But even as she tried to move past it, something remained unsettled. Like a breeze through a cracked window, the awareness stirred now and then, promising to return when least expected. She focused on the street. Rodney was already gone. She hadn't expected him to look back.

But part of her had hoped.

His words echoed in her mind. Perhaps they were nothing more than concern. Or perhaps she was letting her restless thoughts cloud what had always been steady ground.

Still, something sat misaligned in her thoughts, like a portrait hung a little askew. She pressed her hand to the glass. The coolness steadied her.

Her mind wandered to Quinton, not just his sudden return but the quiet strength beneath his silence. He had come back different, subdued. But he was back. That meant something.

Rodney had been here all along. Present. Dependable. Generous.

And yet... something in her heart shifted when she saw Quinton in the foyer. It hadn't been fear. It had been recognition.

She didn't know what to make of it. Not yet. She stepped away from the window, her hand drifting across the bouquet still resting on the table. The petals were soft and lovely, but the perfume clung too tightly now as if overstaying its welcome. Whatever she felt, whatever she feared, it would not be solved today. She didn't need answers now; she only needed the patience to wait for them.

She turned from the window and climbed the stairs slowly, the bouquet in hand. The scent followed her like a memory, faint but unshakable. She entered her bedchamber and found Mrs. Aldridge was already inside, placing folded garments onto the wardrobe shelves.

Mary-Ann set the flowers down on the corner of her writing table.

"Morning, miss," the housekeeper said gently. "I was just seeing to the linens."

"Of course," Mary-Ann replied, calm on the surface, but her pulse had quickened. The wardrobe wasn't safe. Not anymore.

Mrs. Aldridge closed the wardrobe drawer and reached for the flowers. "I'll put them into a vase and bring them back."

"Thank you," Mary-Ann said as she waited for Mrs. Alridge to leave. Once the door closed, she turned the ley in the lock, then opened the wardrobe and retrieved the ledger still tucked safely in her folio beneath the shawls.

She crossed to the far corner of the room, beside her writing desk, where the wainscoting ran low along the outer wall.

Kneeling beside it, just behind the low armchair, where few ever bothered to clean or dust, she found the narrow panel with its familiar warped edge. She had discovered it as a child, a loose seam in the wood where an extra length of trim concealed a shallow cavity.

It had once hidden marbles and pressed flowers. Now, it would serve a greater purpose.

She had found it when she was ten, hiding from a game of

chase with the maids. A knothole caught her skirt, and the loose panel shifted under her fingers. Back then, it had held secrets like feathers, ribbons, and stone marbles. Now, it would hold something far more important.

She opened the wardrobe and pulled the booklet from behind the stack of shawls, clutching it tightly as she knelt beside the wainscoting. She pried the panel open with care and found a long-forgotten tin box. Curious, she opened it and found a button, ribbon, and smooth stones. She slid the folio inside, its cloth cover brushing against the splintered interior, and put the tin box on top. It all fit snugly. She replaced the panel and pressed until the edge caught.

She sat back on her heels and exhaled, a slow, steady breath that grounded her.

She hadn't yet decided what to do with the booklet, not fully. She trusted Quinton. She had always trusted him, even when it had cost her. Rodney… she had trusted him, too. Still did. But something in her, something she couldn't name, had begun to shift.

Maybe it was the wedding.

Maybe it was Quinton's return.

Or maybe, just maybe, it was her.

Chapter Ten

THREE DAYS HAD passed. Now, under a morning drizzle, the house was quiet, but Quinton was already awake. He sat on the edge of the bed in Barrington's guest chamber, running a hand through his hair as he stared at the patterns on the rug. His back ached, not sharply, but with the dull insistence of old bruises and restless sleep. The mattress was far too soft after months of stone and straw, and the silence in the room pressed in from every corner, too polite, too untouched.

Sunlight filtered in through high windows, casting long slats of light across the floor. The morning air carried the scent of lavender soap and the distant clatter of kitchen pans downstairs. Normal sounds. Comfortable sounds. And yet, they made him feel like a ghost walking someone else's life.

A knock at the door, not too loud but precise, brought him back to the present.

"Come in," Quinton called.

Kenworth stepped inside, offering a crisp salute before closing the door behind him. He carried a tray balanced neatly in one hand. "Tea, my lord. And a roll that appears not to have survived the journey."

Quinton managed a faint smile. "Still saluting me, Kenworth? I haven't worn the uniform in years."

Kenworth arched an eyebrow. "Old habits. Also, you tend to sound more reasonable after caffeine."

Quinton accepted the cup. "Thank you."

Kenworth set the tray down on the writing desk and crossed to open the drapes fully. "If I may be so bold, you look slightly less like death than yesterday."

"How comforting." Quinton couldn't help but smile. He and Kenworth had verbally sparred long before the war.

Kenworth tilted his head. "And you haven't bolted yet. That's something."

"Tempting, though," Quinton murmured, sipping the tea. "I don't quite know what to do with myself."

Kenworth's dry voice didn't miss an opportunity. "Perhaps start with putting on trousers. You'll find conversations less drafty that way."

That earned a short, rough, yet real laugh. Quinton shook his head. "You missed your calling."

"I'm still hoping for a promotion to pastry taster, though it may kill me. One more sample of lemon sponge and I shall require an embroidered waistcoat in a larger size. Mrs. Bainbridge keeps sending cakes. It's been a harrowing ordeal."

Quinton chuckled again, but the sound faded. "Did Mary-Ann send word?"

Kenworth hesitated. "No, sir. Not yet."

The silence that followed stretched a little too long.

Quinton looked down into his cup. "She knows I'm here. I sent word. She answered. But still… I don't know what I'd say."

"That you're alive might be a decent start."

Quinton huffed softly. "She has a life now. A future. I'd be stepping into it as the man she once knew, and I'm not sure I'm still him."

Kenworth studied him for a moment, then moved to straighten the edge of the bed cover. "The entire village knows you're back. Letters are being written, hearts aflutter. Mrs. Porter has commissioned a commemorative pudding, and someone has asked Barrington if you'll be giving a speech in the market square. I told him you prefer dramatic cliffside monologues."

"Bloody hell. I hope not."

"But it did make me wonder," Kenworth added lightly, "how the word spread so quickly. Barrington's letter to the Lord Edward in the Home Office only went out two days ago."

The thought lodged sharp and cold.

Quinton's brow furrowed. "You're right. We hadn't even reached Dover when it was posted."

A pause.

Then, quieter: "One of my captors said something strange once. During one of the prisoner exchanges. He told me, *'The post is taken care of.'* I thought he meant the messages were being blocked."

Kenworth's gaze sharpened. "You think it meant something else?"

"I don't know," Quinton said slowly. "But it keeps echoing back. Especially after what you just said."

Kenworth didn't reply, but the air between them shifted.

He began to gather the breakfast tray then paused. "You're not thinking of going to her, are you?"

Quinton didn't answer at first. Then, very quietly, he said, "I told myself I would. But now, I don't know."

Kenworth's voice softened. "You're not the only one who's changed."

Quinton turned toward the window. The morning sunlight was bright on the stone paths. Too bright. Everything was orderly, gentle, and clean. It clashed with what he had carried back.

"She looked beautiful," he said suddenly.

Kenworth didn't need clarification. "She always did."

Quinton smiled, but it didn't reach his eyes. That smile, her smile. Not rehearsed. Not polite. And in that moment, the years he'd lost, the words he'd never sent, the ache he'd carried, it all surged back.

God, it hit him like a blow. There she was, the memory and the woman, converging in a single moment that made the distance between them stretch sharper than any prison bar. Years he couldn't get back. Words he never got to send. All of it knotted in that smile. "She smiled at me. That's what undid me."

"It usually does."

Quinton leaned against the frame. "I don't know what I expected. I knew she'd be changed. But I hoped… maybe I hoped I'd still see the way she used to look at me. That I could still be the man she saw then."

"And do you think she still sees that man?"

Quinton shook his head. "Not yet. Maybe not ever. But she was the reason I held on. I used to count the days, thinking she was counting them too."

He paused, his voice softer now.

"When I was in that cell, there was a crack in the stone wall, just wide enough to see a strip of sky. Some days, it was gray. Some days, it burned blue. Sometimes, when the light shifted just so, I could see the shadow of birds passing overhead. It reminded me that the world was still moving, even when I couldn't. And I used to imagine what she'd say about it. Sometimes, it was something trivial, her opinion on the sky's color, the proper number of teaspoons for tea, or whether she'd ever seen a storm roll in like that. But other days, she asked me how I was holding on. And on the worst nights, I'd pretend she was reading to me. That soft, steady voice kept the dark at bay. I made up conversations with her. It helped me keep my mind from slipping."

Kenworth stepped back, gentler now. "You're not the only one who's changed."

Quinton looked over. "I know. I saw it in her eyes. She's not waiting to be rescued."

"Which makes her worth the effort."

The words struck deeper than they should have. Quinton nodded slowly.

"Eat the roll," Kenworth said on his way out. "A man can't win back a woman on half a breakfast and a brooding expression."

But when the door clicked shut behind Kenworth, the quiet pressed in again. Quinton looked around the room, taking in the carved wardrobe, the patterned carpet, and the book left askew on the side table. All of it should have felt comforting.

None of it was his.

His mind circled the conversation, Wilkinson, the letters, the crack in the wall, and Mary-Ann's voice in his memory. She had been more than a beacon. Mary-Ann had been his anchor. The way she tilted her head when she asked a question, the spark of mischief in her eyes when she teased him. He had held on to those fragments like lifelines.

And now? Now she was real again. And real was not a memory or a prayer. It was messy, uncertain, and full of edges.

A knock came again, sharper this time, and snapped Quinton from his spiral of thought. The moment dissolved. The room, the world, shifted. He flinched before he could stop himself, his breath catching tight in his chest. Too many nights had trained him to brace for what waited behind a door. But this wasn't that place. Not anymore. He drew a slow breath. This time, it was Barrington.

"We have something," he said without preamble as he stepped in. "A message from one of Edward's old contacts. Meet me in the study when you're ready."

Quinton nodded.

As he dressed, he moved slowly, not because of pain but because of what waited in the next room. The war he'd survived wasn't over. It had only changed shape.

He buttoned his coat, catching sight of himself in the dressing mirror. His reflection was thinner, his eyes shadowed, but his spine was straight. The man in the mirror looked older. Not just thinner, not just tired, but forged. Like something that had been through fire and returned harder, quieter.

Whatever this is, I'm not broken.

His hand paused briefly on the latch.

This battlefield would demand something else entirely, cleverness, patience, and the kind of courage that didn't wear medals. And at the center of it all was…

Mary-Ann.

Chapter Eleven

TUESDAY AFTERNOON, THE hour before Mrs. Bainbridge's weekly tea, Mary-Ann adjusted her shawl as she stepped up the front path to the Sommer-by-the-Sea Female Seminary. The morning was crisp, with a faint salt breeze drifting in from the sea. She clutched a slim folder of papers, figures from one of Mrs. Bainbridge's students whom she'd been asked to evaluate. It was a welcome distraction, one she had embraced eagerly. Numbers made sense in a way people no longer did.

Inside, the entry hall smelled of chalk dust and lemon polish. Laughter, the sharp crack of a ruler, the scrape of chairs against the wood, all familiar sounds, drifted from one of the classrooms. The comforting normalcy of it all wrapped around her like a balm.

She paused a moment longer than necessary, letting her hand trail along the wainscoting. She used to run her fingers along these same grooves as a girl, tracing the path to the mathematics room where she'd begged for extra problems just to stay a little longer. Numbers were safer than people then. Predictable. Kind. She remembered walking these halls and the nervous thrill of receiving a corrected paper with high marks, and the way Mrs. Bainbridge would tilt her head just so when offering praise. There had been safety in those early years, in the structure and certainty of numbers and expectations. The world beyond the seminary walls had felt simpler then, more distant.

Mrs. Bainbridge emerged from her office at the end of the

corridor, spectacles perched on her nose and a stack of letters in her hand. "Mary-Ann," she said with a warm smile, "you're a welcome sight. Come in, come in."

They stepped into the office, and Mrs. Bainbridge shut the door behind them. The room was lined with shelves of books and student records, the desk piled with notes and the inevitable teacup. A vase of early spring flowers brightened the windowsill.

Mary-Ann set the folder down gently. "I finished reviewing your student's figures. She's brilliant. There's a precision to her work, and she's clearly testing formulas beyond the lesson. If she continues at this pace, she could qualify for advanced training."

Mrs. Bainbridge beamed. "I thought you'd say so. She reminded me of someone else who used to spend all their time with numbers."

Mary-Ann flushed slightly. "You're far too kind."

"Only accurate," Mrs. Bainbridge said firmly. "You had a gift. You still do."

There was a pause, comfortable and close.

"And how are you?" The headmistress asked, her tone softening. "Truly."

Mary-Ann hesitated. She looked down at her hands. "I'm… unsettled. Everything I thought was behind me isn't. And I don't know what to do with that."

Bainbridge studied her a moment. "It's all right not to know."

Mary-Ann gave a faint, grateful smile. "Thank you."

Bainbridge sat on the edge of her desk and motioned for Mary-Ann to do the same. "It must be strange. Seeing someone you once loved walk back into your life like that."

Mary-Ann huffed a laugh, though her expression was sober. "It wasn't supposed to happen. I'd mourned him. Let him go. And now I feel as though I'm betraying something, someone, no matter what I choose."

Mrs. Bainbridge leaned forward. "You're not betraying anyone. Grief and healing are not betrayals. They're survival. You did what you had to."

Mary-Ann looked away, her eyes burning. "I don't know how to look him in the eye and pretend I'm not torn in two."

"Then don't pretend," Mrs. Bainbridge said. "But don't run, either."

The door opened slightly, and a student peeked in. Mrs. Bainbridge excused herself with a promise of tea and stepped out.

Left alone, Mary-Ann wandered to the windows, grateful for the moment of stillness. A pair of gulls wheeled overhead in the sky. She let her thoughts drift, to Quinton's voice, to Wilkinson's visit, to the ledger hidden behind the wainscoting, silent, damning, patient, as if waiting for her courage to match her suspicion. She didn't know which unsettled her more, the past, the present, or the quiet feeling that the two were about to collide.

Her gaze fell on the playground beyond the hedge. A cluster of students played at sums with chalk and slates, arguing over a solution with the same vigor others might apply to a game of hoops. She smiled faintly. Once, that had been her.

Watching the girls jostle and scribble as if every number held the key to victory, she saw more than sums. Some played by the rules, careful and exact, like Rodney. Others pushed boundaries and dared mistakes as Quinton had always done. She remembered how he once changed the rules of a card game mid-play just to make her laugh. He'd always been unpredictable, infuriating, irresistible. Both approaches had merit. But only one had ever stirred her heart.

But only one had ever stirred her heart.

Behind her, the door opened again. Mrs. Bainbridge returned with a folded paper in one hand.

"The London Gazette," she said, offering it to Mary-Ann. "Barrington insisted I see it, and now I'm inflicting it on you."

Mary-Ann unfolded it and read the notice aloud. "Commander Barrington and Mrs. Honoria Bainbridge are pleased to announce their engagement." She looked up, grinning. "It's real now."

Mrs. Bainbridge rolled her eyes. "Don't tell him, but I kept a second copy for framing."

"You must be very happy."

"I am," Mrs. Bainbridge said, then added wryly, "in between cake tastings and interrogations about the guest list."

Mary-Ann laughed, and for the first time in days, it felt genuine.

"Have you begun choosing your gown?" she teased.

"I've narrowed it down to two. Which is to say, I'm precisely where I was a week ago."

"Perhaps I should help. I seem to be excelling at stalling decisions lately."

Mrs. Bainbridge gave her a look that was more motherly than amused. "Some decisions need time. Others need courage."

A footman arrived with a small tray of tea. As Bainbridge reached for the teapot, she paused and opened the drawer of her desk. From it, she withdrew a pale cream envelope.

"I received this at the house this morning," she said, offering it to Mary-Ann, who read it quickly. "It's an invitation to the charity dinner next week. Half the town will be there. I expect Quinton will be there as well."

Mary-Ann reached inside her reticule. "I received one as well," she said softly, withdrawing a similar envelope from her reticule. Her name was written in a familiar copperplate hand. She hadn't meant to feel it, the flutter low in her belly at the thought of Quinton, but there it was. Unexpected. And utterly real.

She hadn't opened it, not because she feared the contents, but because it was easier not to name what she wasn't ready to face.

Mrs. Bainbridge poured the tea without comment, though her eyes flicked once to Mary-Ann's.

"Rodney will be there, too," Mrs. Bainbridge said, watching her carefully.

Mary-Ann didn't answer.

Mrs. Bainbridge softened her voice. "You don't have to decide anything now. But sometimes showing up is the first step to knowing where you stand."

Mary-Ann nodded slowly. She held the invite as she glanced out the window again, her heart still heavy, but not quite so numb. She didn't know what choice, not yet, but she was beginning to admit the question had to be faced. But she was no longer pretending she didn't have one.

She sat for a few moments longer, turning the card over in her hand. The smooth surface of the paper was a strange weight. It was more than parchment and ink. It held expectations. Her name seemed to taunt her with what she hadn't yet faced.

She pictured Rodney greeting her with that practiced charm, perfectly pleasant and entirely composed. She imagined Quinton, quiet but watchful, standing somewhere near the edge of the room as if unsure whether he belonged. It would be easy to slip into a routine with Rodney. Easy to wear the smile expected of her. But the thought made her chest ache in a way that had nothing to do with grief.

She slipped the invitation carefully into her reticule as if hiding it might buy her more time.

Mrs. Bainbridge poured the tea and handed her a cup. "I suppose next week will be interesting."

Mary-Ann allowed herself a small laugh. "In this village, everything is interesting."

They sipped in silence for a while.

Finally, Mrs. Bainbridge said, "If you come to dinner, I suspect you'll know more by the end of it than you do now."

Mary-Ann met her gaze and nodded slowly. "And if I don't?"

Mrs. Bainbridge smiled gently. "Then you'll still be exactly where you are. And that's fine, for now."

Mary-Ann held the teacup in both hands, letting the warmth seep into her fingers. "One step at a time."

"Exactly."

The breeze had picked up outside, tugging gently at the curtains. She stood after a few more quiet minutes and gathered her things. "Thank you for tea."

"Thank you," Mrs. Bainbridge said as she walked her to the door, "for looking over the paper and giving me your evaluation."

Outside, the air was brisk, the kind that carried both salt and promise. The future wasn't clear, not yet, but it waited with open arms.

She paused on the step, letting the wind tug at her shawl, her gaze lifting to the distant line of the sea. Somewhere beyond the rooftops, waves rolled in without hesitation. She wasn't ready to be swept away, but perhaps she was ready to stop standing still.

She took a breath and stepped forward.

Chapter Twelve

WEDNESDAY MORNING, UNDER a pale sky that held its breath in quiet anticipation, Quinton found Barrington in the study, already seated behind his desk with a folded sheet of thick parchment before him like a verdict waiting to be read. The morning light cast a warm glow across the desk's polished surface. It was quiet except for the faint tick of the mantle clock and the distant call of gulls beyond the windows.

"You said there was news," Quinton said as he entered.

Barrington gestured to the chair opposite. "From one of Edward's contacts. This concerns your captivity, and the silence surrounding it. This came by courier before breakfast."

Quinton sat as Barrington unfolded the letter.

"They've uncovered a cache of undelivered letters," Barrington said. "Discovered in the back room of a shuttered coaching inn in Suffolk. Evidently, the place served as a temporary holding station during the war when the roads were impassable. Some of the bags were forgotten or never sent forward."

Quinton frowned. "How many letters?"

"Hundreds. Perhaps more. Most from five or six years ago, wartime dispatches. Family correspondence, military reports, and personal notes. Some addressed to soldiers, others to their families."

He pushed Edward's letter across the desk. "The majority were water-damaged, but a few were legible. Nothing directly connected to us. Not yet. But the team is still reviewing them."

Quinton scanned the document. The contact, someone identified only by initials, mentioned additional caches found in nearby towns. A pattern, perhaps.

He imagined what the paper might feel like, softened by time, curled at the corners, the ink smudged by dampness and neglect. What if his name was there? Or hers? He didn't dare hope, but the hunger to look was already there, sharp and familiar.

One that had gone unseen for years.

"Edward's working quietly," Barrington said. "He doesn't want to alert anyone until we know how widespread it is."

Quinton leaned back in the chair, his brow furrowed. "When I was in the camp, I overheard one of the guards say that the post was taken care of. At the time, I thought it meant no one had sent word or that it was merely a casual comment. Or that the mail has been intercepted or destroyed. But now, I'm not so certain."

Barrington's expression turned grim. "It might have meant more than you thought."

Quinton looked at the letter again, at the dates and places scrawled in tight, rushed script. This wasn't about anyone else. Not Mary-Ann, not the others left waiting. This was about him. About silence so complete it had nearly erased him. One of the mailbags had originated from a nearby town, no more than a day's ride from Sommer-by-the-Sea.

"If my family had received word I was alive—"

Barrington cut in gently. "You can't think that way."

But Quinton's voice remained steady. "If they had, they would have written. And Mary-Ann... she would have known. She would have waited."

Silence fell between them.

Quinton turned to look out the window. A fishing boat drifted across the morning tide, the sails sharp against the pale sky.

"They buried me," he said. "Not literally, but close enough. And they mourned me. All because someone failed, or chose not, to deliver a letter."

Barrington set his cup down with a little more force than

necessary. He didn't speak right away. Instead, he crossed to the window, his back to Quinton, his jaw tight. "We trusted the system," he said at last. "But someone manipulated it. That ends now."

He had a way of speaking in absolutes. He was calm, reasoning, and never careless. But even now, Quinton saw the tension in his jaw, the barely masked concern that mirrored his own.

Quinton nodded. "And if it wasn't a failure? If it was deliberate?"

"Then we follow the trail. Quietly."

Barrington reached for the teapot on the sideboard and poured two cups. The gesture was domestic, steadying.

Edward's contact believes that someone may have intentionally rerouted or withheld certain letters. He has reason to believe this wasn't an isolated case."

Quinton accepted the tea but didn't drink it. His fingers curled around the warmth.

"How many people vanished without a word, without explanation? How many loved ones never knew what became of them?"

There had been one man, O'Dell. He was quiet and kind, with his eyes always fixed on the horizon. He'd stopped talking after the second winter. No word had ever come for him. They found him curled against the wall one morning, cold and still. Quinton had wondered, later, if a single letter could have saved him."

"Too many." Barrington's voice was barely a whisper.

The warmth of the tea seeped into his palms, grounding him. Quinton let the silence linger, unsure whether it soothed or strained him. The silence had once been a torment, too loud, too long. He had strained to hear footsteps, voices, even the wind through the stone, anything to prove the world still moved beyond his cell. Now, even in safety, it followed him like a shadow. The damp in the walls had carried mildew and iron, a constant reminder of where he was and what he was losing. In a moment of quiet, his mind returned to the prison walls, to the scratch of stone beneath his fingers, and the desperation of remembering names, places, anything to keep the darkness at bay. Letters would have been salvation. A name, a scrap of handwriting, would have given him something to hold onto.

"I used to imagine letters coming," he said after a moment. "That someone out there still believed in me. I made up entire conversations with Mary-Ann. It kept me sane.

"I imagined her handwriting, neat, precise, always slanting slightly to the left. Her letters began, *My dearest Quinton*, and always ended, *Yours, until you return*. I used to whisper them aloud at night, just to remember what it felt like to be wanted, to be known."

Barrington's voice was softer now. "It wasn't your imagination. She never stopped hoping. Not until hope had nowhere left to go."

The words caught something raw inside him. He didn't respond.

Then Barrington cleared his throat and stood. "There's a dinner next week. A charity event. You'll receive an invitation soon."

Quinton glanced at him. "And she'll be there."

"Likely."

"Do you think I should go?"

Barrington shrugged. "Do you want to see her again?"

Quinton looked down into the cup. "I don't know. I mean, yes. But I don't know if I can face what I lost."

"Then go. Don't speak if you're not ready. But don't avoid it, either."

Quinton gave a faint smile. "You sound like Mrs. Bainbridge."

"We've all been listening to her long enough to learn a thing or two."

Quinton stood and glanced out the window. The sea was calm, the morning deceptively serene. He rested his hand on the frame.

"If the truth is buried in these letters," he said quietly, "then I intend to read every one of them."

Barrington nodded, the quiet oath settling between them like smoke.

As he turned to leave, Barrington paused beside him. His hand landed briefly on Quinton's shoulder, steady, silent enough. Then he turned away without waiting for thanks.

Later, in the solitude of his room, Quinton sat at the writing desk. The letter from Barrington's contact lay beside a blank sheet of paper. He picked up a pen but didn't write.

Outside, the world continued its quiet rhythm. But something had shifted.

He had been forgotten once. He would not let it happen again, not to himself, and not to her.

He set the pen down and pushed the letter aside. His eyes drifted to the edge of the desk, where a faint scratch in the wood caught the light. It reminded him of the crude markings carved into the stone wall of his cell, tallies of days, names of men, fragments of memory etched in desperation. He had nothing left from those years but scars and recollections, yet they had become as real as any object he could hold.

He leaned back in his chair, eyes closing briefly. There had been no books, no flowers, no comfort. Only silence and what he could summon from within. The soft lilt of Mary-Ann's voice. The curve of her smile. He remembered one summer evening. Mary-Ann was reading aloud by lamplight, stumbling over a word only to laugh and make up a new one entirely. That laugh had stayed with him longer than any scripture or sermon.

They had come to him not as ghosts but as lifelines. He didn't need relics to remember her. He didn't need pages or portraits. She was there, stitched into his memory with a thread no time could fray. He had remembered despite everything.

If she had waited, if the letter had come, would they already be married? Would he have avoided the long nights filled with nothing but stone and silence?

He shook the thought away. The truth was, they were both changed. But perhaps the pieces still fit, just differently than before.

He stood and crossed to the small washstand, splashing cool water on his face. The simple ritual helped him shake loose the weight of reflection, though it didn't lighten the pressure in his chest. As he reached for a towel, he caught sight of his own face in the mirror, a face that bore shadows deeper than time could smooth. There was a pale streak near his temple that hadn't been there before. A ghost of the years he'd lived but not lived through.

There were moments in the prison camp when he hadn't expected to see his own reflection again. He'd prepared himself for death more than once, and when hope faded, it was the memory of Mary-Ann's laughter, bright, sudden, impossible to bottle, that had called him back.

He no longer looked like the man who'd left for war. There was steel in his jaw now and quiet defiance in his eyes. He had faced silence, starvation, and solitude and survived. This wasn't a return. It was a reckoning. And if the world expected him to pick up his old life as though nothing had changed, they would be mistaken. He would not simply drift back into place.

There were questions to ask and truths to uncover. And somewhere, woven between every silence, every unanswered letter, every breath he'd fought to hold, was Mary-Ann.

He returned to the desk and picked up the pen again, holding it above the blank page. Not yet. But soon. Because he wasn't about to let the silence that had once swallowed him do it again.

Not while there were still words to speak. Not while Mary-Ann remained part of the story that was unfinished.

Chapter Thirteen

T HAT EVENING, AS twilight softly draped the land, they approached the castle. Sommer Castle, with its towering arched windows and weathered stone walls, had stood vacant for generations until the town of Sommer-by-the-Sea reclaimed it for public gatherings. The soft golden light poured from its many windows as footmen flanked the arched entry, guiding guests into the great hall beyond. The castle's cavernous interior had been transformed. Heavy floral arrangements perfumed the air, tables were set with polished silver and crystal, and musicians from Brighton played in the gallery above the stairs.

Quinton stood just inside the main entrance, adjusting the cuffs of his coat. He hadn't attended a proper dinner in years, and the formality of the setting felt almost foreign. He took in the high, vaulted ceiling and the sheen of hundreds of candles. Against the backdrop of laughter and music, he felt oddly removed, as though he watched from the edge of someone else's memory.

He was deliberately early. He had learned, during his years away, that control was often found in the quiet moments before chaos began. He scanned the crowd, searching for nothing and everything. His pulse quickened despite himself.

A pair of officers passed near the entrance, pausing to greet a cluster of older gentlemen by the brandy station. One of them, tall and silver-haired at the temples, with an easy manner and a distinct military posture, shook hands with the mayor and clapped a steward on the back.

"Colonel Gideon Rathbone," Barrington said beside him, noting Quinton's glance. "Retired now. Served with distinction in the Channel squadrons. One of the few Ordnance men people still trust."

Quinton nodded faintly, unable to place the name, though the voice stirred something distant. "Seems well liked."

"He is," Barrington said. "And loyal to the last. I wish we had more like him. They've done well with the castle," he said as he glanced around. "I remember when this place was home to nothing but bats."

Quinton gave a faint smile. "It still feels more suited to armor and ghosts."

Barrington chuckled. "And yet here we are, drinking claret and supporting lifeboats."

"All this for lifeboats," Quinton murmured, scanning the floral arrangements and polished silver.

Barrington huffed a quiet laugh. "The Lifeboat Trust was the matrons' doing. A trio of sharp-eyed women with a gift for stirring hearts and emptying pockets. Don't let their lace gloves fool you. They could fund a fleet if they chose."

"Is it working?"

"Tonight's meant to restore the rescue skiffs and train more volunteers. After the last storm, they decided Sommer-by-the-Sea needed better protection." He gestured at the crowded room. "Judging by the attendance, they were right. The castle isn't used often, but when it is, the attendance proves them right."

"You'll see Professor Tresham tonight," Barrington added. "The mathematician from Oxford. He's here to support the trust's academic scholarship fund."

Quinton glanced at the crowd. "Will Mrs. Bainbridge be here tonight?"

Barrington gave a resigned nod. "Most definitely. The matrons placed her at the center of their seating chart. Something about honoring 'local academic heroines.'"

"And Mary-Ann?"

"Honoria mentioned that she accepted the invitation. That's all I know."

Quinton looked toward the grand staircase, where new arrivals were being announced. The press of movement stirred something tense in his chest. It was one thing to think of her. it was another to see her again.

Guests arrived in elegant succession. The ladies in silks and satins and the gentlemen in tailcoats. They all nodded graciously as they were announced. It was a sea of cordial smiles and clipped conversation. He was casting an eye over the crowd when the air shifted, and his attention was drawn back to the grand staircase.

"Miss Mary-Ann Seaton." Her name was announced before she moved to the top of the staircase.

The sight of her knocked something loose in his chest. For a moment, he could barely process the room around her. All he noticed was the way her gown shifted with each step and the soft candlelight warming her skin.

He had seen her once, the day he returned. Held her hand. But the moment had been brief and staggering, more confusion than clarity. Since then, they had stayed apart, each unsure of what the other carried.

Now, with time slowed and no one interrupting, he saw her fully, and it undid him.

A rush of memories cascaded through him, her laughter carried on the wind, her ink-stained fingers as she worked over account books, and the feeling of her hand wrapped in his before he left. All of it returned, sharper than any dream.

He hadn't realized how long he'd been holding his breath for this moment to come again, and how much it terrified him.

His gloved hand tightened at his side.

She wore a soft celadon gown with delicate embroidery along the hem. Her hair was swept back in loose waves, pinned with tiny pearls. She carried herself with quiet confidence, but her eyes darted briefly over the crowd, searching. Quinton stayed where he was, half-shadowed by a marble pillar. She hadn't seen him...yet.

He didn't move. Didn't breathe. Just watched.

She was more beautiful than he remembered. Not because time had altered her. The memory he'd carried through the darkest nights hadn't failed him. It had simply fallen short of her true beauty.

She turned slightly, offering her arm to Mrs. Bainbridge, who had arrived at her side. They moved deeper into the room, only to be intercepted quickly by well-wishers. Quinton stayed rooted in place.

"Are you planning to speak with her," Barrington asked, "or haunt her from the shadows all evening?"

Quinton gave a quiet huff. "I haven't decided."

"If you wait too long, Wilkinson will get there first."

Before Quinton could respond, Mr. Rodney Wilkinson was announced.

He entered with a confident smile, his coat tailored and his hair too perfect. He moved with ease through the room, stopping to greet acquaintances as his gaze swept the crowd. It landed on Mary-Ann.

Quinton watched as Rodney approached her. Her smile was pleasant and polite. Wilkinson leaned in to say something. Her expression didn't falter, but her shoulders shifted ever so slightly. That small movement burned itself into Quinton's mind.

"Still not sure?" Barrington asked.

Quinton stepped away from the pillar. "No. I'm sure now."

They didn't speak again until they reached the refreshment table. Barrington took a slow sip of his drink while Quinton's eyes followed Mary-Ann across the room. "You don't have to say anything," he said without turning. "But I was there when she got the last letter. I've never seen a woman read so many lines that weren't written."

Quinton didn't answer. He didn't have to.

After a pause, Barrington nodded toward the far wall.

"Did you hear the story in today's *Sentinel*?"

Quinton raised a brow.

"Children were playing down by the western caves," Barrington said. "The tide came in faster than expected. They were pulled out safely, but the situation has sparked renewed discussion. People forget how dangerous those cave tunnels are."

Quinton sipped his wine. "We used to play in those caves. I'd forgotten how fast the tide can shift."

Barrington gave him a sidelong glance. "The tide's always shifting, Quinton. Best to keep your footing."

Quinton glanced at Wilkinson, then gave Barrington a tight smile. "Noted."

Dinner was announced shortly after. Quinton took his place at a table near the center.

There would be no formal withdrawal tonight. Lady Trowbridge, one of three matrons of the event, had insisted that keeping the guests mingling would encourage more spontaneous generosity. "Dancing raises donations," she'd quipped, and the matrons had adopted the approach with enthusiasm.

To his surprise, and perhaps to someone's design, Mary-Ann was seated directly across from him. She met his gaze. And held it.

A thousand words passed between them in silence. Her eyes flicked down, then back to his. A question. A challenge. A memory.

He could feel her gaze like the warmth of a fire, present, flickering, impossible to ignore. It was both comfort and torment. Until now, he'd made himself stay away, out of respect, or duty, or the knowledge that she belonged to another. But tonight, he didn't want distance. He wanted to remember what no memory could fully hold.

He inclined his head slightly. She returned the gesture.

Rodney took the seat beside her and began to speak, but Quinton couldn't hear the words. He didn't need to.

Rodney leaned in, just a touch too familiar. He gestured

broadly with his hand, an affectation Quinton had forgotten, but now found it irritating. Mary-Ann's expression remained composed, but a flicker of emotion crossed her eyes, a momentary glance downward before she smiled. He knew that look. She was shielding something. Or someone.

The first course was served. Something with poached fish and saffron. Quinton barely touched it. The sounds of silverware and polite laughter filled the hall, but his focus narrowed to the woman across the table from him.

Mary-Ann smiled when addressed. She nodded at the appropriate comments. But once or twice, she looked his way again.

And when she did, it wasn't just a polite acknowledgment. It was recognition, the kind that stirred a low heat in his chest. His hand tightened around his wineglass. He should look away. But he couldn't, nor did he want to, because whatever passed between them wasn't indifference.

After the final course was cleared and a toast made to the Lifeboat Trust's renewed mission, the guests began rising from the tables. Conversations trailed like ribbons behind them as they made their way back to the ballroom.

A string ensemble resumed in the adjoining hall, striking the first notes of a country dance as the castle staff moved deftly to guide the transition. The Lifeboat Trust matrons lingered at the doors, ushering everyone along with satisfied expressions. Dancing, after all, meant prolonged generosity.

Quinton leaned back slightly, watching as the first dancers took to the floor. Once, in another lifetime, he might have claimed her hand without hesitation. The swell of violins struck a chord in his chest. He used to imagine this, her hand in his, the sweep of her dress, the thrill of leading her into something light. But that dream had been too tender to hold in the dark. So he'd buried it. During his captivity, in the endless days and nights, he'd stare at the stars through slits in the stone wall where the mortar had worn away. He imagined it, dancing with her, hand in hand. And now, here she was. Real. Yet out of reach.

Barrington leaned over. "Will you dance with her?"

Quinton shook his head slowly. "Not yet."

Barrington snorted. "You're going to make her do it, aren't you?"

Quinton smiled faintly. "Make her? No. She never needed prompting before."

Mary-Ann stepped aside to speak with Mrs. Bainbridge. Even across the room, he noticed something guarded in her posture, as if she felt his gaze. She turned once, not toward him, but toward the crowd, her glance sweeping past where he stood. Was she looking for him? He couldn't be sure. But she didn't look fully at ease. Her smile was pleasant but carefully composed. Her hands were still. Then she turned again and saw him.

Before she could gather herself, he was approaching her. His steps were sure, unhurried as he approached her from the side. She turned before he spoke.

"Quinton." Her voice was even, but her eyes searched his face.

"Mary-Ann." He nodded, his eyes twinkling.

They stood in silence for a breath.

"You look well," she said.

He accepted the compliment with a quiet nod. "So do you."

She didn't respond to that. Not directly.

"I was hoping you'd be here," she said softly, surprising them both.

She glanced away for a moment, then added more lightly, "Everyone's glad you're home."

He tilted his head. "And you?"

Her eyes met his again, steady this time. "Yes. Me too."

He hadn't expected calm acceptance nor the warmth beneath it. The quiet, undeniable truth that he still matters to her.

"Will you walk with me?" he asked.

HER BREATH CAUGHT just slightly, and she hesitated. Something passed through her expression. It was quick and unspoken before she nodded. Still, clarity had always steadied her. If she had questions, this was how she would get answers. "Yes," she said. And threaded her arm through his.

They slipped toward the edge of the room into a narrow corridor where the music faded to a distant hum. She didn't know why she'd said yes. Not exactly. Her feet had moved before her mind had caught up. But now, with his arm so close, the distance between what had been and what might still be felt narrower than ever. It wasn't forgiveness she sought. It was something quieter, a kind of knowing. And in that corridor, with no music and no audience, she might find it.

Their arms barely touched, linen brushing wool, but the contact was enough to root him. The warmth of her beside him, real, not imagined, stilled everything else.

The air was cooler there, and the stone walls carried echoes of their footsteps. Mary-Ann ran her fingers along the wall, trailing them across the ridges. Quinton watched her silently, struck by how naturally she moved through this space as if it belonged to her. Candle sconces flickered along the way, casting golden pools of light and long shadows across the stone floor. The scent of beeswax and old stone lingered in the air, earthy, quiet, a world apart from the laughter and strings behind them.

"You've changed," she said softly.

He nodded. "So have you."

"I don't know what to say when I look at you."

"Say what's true." He looked ahead.

"That you still brood too much?" she said, the familiar lilt hitting him like a memory made flesh.

The corner of his mouth twitched. It was something she used to tease him about, and hearing it now, nestled among tension and truth, it made his chest tighten. She remembered. Not just the man, but their language. The private vocabulary that only two people in love could invent.

She paused. "I'm glad you're alive," she said softly.

He looked at her, searching for something beyond her words. "That's enough." And it was for now.

As they walked on, the silence between them wasn't empty. It carried years of what was unsaid.

"Do you ever think," she began, "that if one letter had found its way through, just one, we'd be in an entirely different situation?"

He met her eyes. "I used to think that every day."

She nodded once, sharply. "So did I."

She glanced at him again, and for a moment, it was as if the silence between them gave way. Not enemies. Not strangers. Just two people who had waited too long, each believing the other had let go.

The moment stretched, long and fragile.

Behind them, the music swelled as the orchestra changed tempo.

"I should go back," she said.

He stepped aside. "Of course."

She didn't move immediately. She glanced back, not quite at him, but in his direction. Her fingers brushed the wall before she stepped back through the archway into the ballroom.

She didn't look back. But something in her bearing had shifted. He couldn't name it exactly. Only that the distance between them no longer felt impassable.

Quinton remained behind. He didn't follow. Not yet.

The notes of the waltz drifted faintly down the corridor. His footsteps echoed softly and distinctly as if even the air around him had chosen silence.

He ran a hand along the cool stone wall, tracing hers. He exhaled. The tension hadn't left him, but it had shifted. She remembered him, their past, the language that had once been theirs alone.

That was more than enough. He'd lost her once, and it had nearly ruined him. He would not lose her to silence again.

He didn't come tonight to make decisions. But the moment she met his eyes across the ballroom when she spoke in the rhythm only they had shared, the course had set itself.

He would make her love him again. Not by pleading. Not by pressing. But by reminding her of everything they had once been and everything they still could be.

His mission was set.

Chapter Fourteen

THURSDAY MORNING, THE crisp coastal fog enveloped the day in quiet mystery. The door to her father's study clicked softly behind her. Mary-Ann paused for a moment, letting the hush of the room settle over her. This space had always felt more formal than familiar, lined with ledgers, brass navigation instruments, oil portraits of ships no longer sailing. A place of precision and decisions. Yet now, it felt less like a monument and more like a question.

She crossed to the desk, her fingertips trailing lightly along its edge. The ledger she'd worked through the previous week still sat on the side, its spine facing out. She had returned not for it specifically but because she couldn't sleep. Because Quinton's voice still echoed in her mind, and the sight of Rodney's knowing smile over last night's dinner haunted her more than she wanted to admit.

She reached toward the desk drawer to retrieve a fresh sheet of paper when her gaze caught on something nestled between a pair of wooden bookends on the shelf above. A small piece of carved whalebone sat unobtrusively beside a sea glass paper-weight.

She drew the whalebone down gently.

The bone was smoothed from years of handling, its surface etched with the careful design of a ship's wheel, just like the one she remembered.

"Wren," she whispered.

He'd been one of Hamish's longest-serving men. A quiet sailor, thoughtful more than shy. He rarely spoke in meetings but always brought his reports in early, sometimes tied with twine. Once, he had given her a carved shell, saying the tide left it just for her. He had died months ago of a worsening cough that no one, not even Dr. Manning, had thought was dangerous.

She sat down, the bone still in hand, and pulled the old ledger closer. Her breath slowed as she opened the back cover. The same weight, the same scent, faint salt, ink, time. The pages felt heavier than before. She didn't need to see more. Not yet.

She rose from the desk and, with the ledger tucked carefully beneath her arm, she crossed the hall and went up the grand stairs to her bedroom.

Inside, the familiar hush wrapped around her like a wool blanket. She shut the door behind her, put the ledger on her desk, and then went straight to the small seam in the wainscoting. Her fingertips easily found the hidden groove. With a gentle push, the panel gave way. She reached into the narrow hollow and pulled free the cloth-bound booklet.

Mary-Ann sat at her desk, opened the booklet, and studied the symbols, marks, and ship names. She found notations that seemed out of place, coded, and impatiently written. Her heart picked up pace as she turned around.

There, peaking over the edge of the top edge of the page, like a bookmark, was something she hadn't noticed before. A scrap of paper, roughly torn. The ink had bled slightly across the grain. The hand was not Hamish's.

She read the words once. Then again.

Don't trust the man with clean hands.

It wasn't a signature. It wasn't a plea. It was a warning.

Her breath caught.

She didn't know the hand, not with certainty. The script was tight and slanted, hurried. Not Hamish's. Not familiar. But deliberately hidden, like something someone wanted to be found only by the right eyes.

Had he known? Had he tried to tell someone? Had Hamish kept the message, not to hide it, but to preserve it? For her?

She thought of Hamish's voice, low and steady, reading aloud from shipping logs as if they were scripture. Of nights, she'd curled near the fire while he debated routes with her father over brandy and biscuits. Once, she'd heard them say a name, Galen or Garrity, she couldn't remember, and her father's voice had dropped. She hadn't understood it then. She wondered if she would now.

She sank into the chair at her desk. The paper fluttered slightly in her grasp. She folded the paper once, carefully, and tucked it into the small pocket of her reticule. She would carry it with her and begin asking the right questions until she knew what it meant and to whom it was intended.

She didn't have answers. Not yet. But she was no longer standing in the dark. She pressed her fingers to the edge of the paper. Not Hamish's hand. But maybe his intent. He'd died protecting something. Now she wondered if Wren had, too. Not men who shouted or commanded, but men who watched, who carried burdens quietly. She had learned to trust them before she ever understood why. Now she felt their absence like missing stars on a chart. The kind that pointed to something larger.

She returned briefly to the study, the silence there thicker than before. The whalebone still rested where she had left it on the edge of her father's desk. She didn't touch it this time, only looked at it long enough to wonder whether her father had ever questioned where it came from or if he simply assumed everything had its place. She stood in the hush of wood-paneled certainty, where numbers and maps told clean stories and felt for the first time that perhaps this room had never been built for questions.

❯❯❯◀◀◀

Quinton had always risen early, but this morning he had been awake long before the first light touched the windows. The house was quiet; the world was still, hushed with a kind of stillness that demanded reflection. He welcomed it.

Kenworth had appeared only briefly, bearing tea and a raised brow. "You've been pacing since dawn, my lord. Shall I lay out walking boots or war plans?" He set the tray down with the quiet efficiency of a man long resigned to eccentric masters.

Quinton hadn't answered at first. His posture was still, but tension coiled at his shoulders like a tether that had been held too long. There was no plan yet. Not one he'd settled on.

He stood now near the window of the guest room with one hand braced against the frame as he looked out over Barrington's well-kept garden. Beyond it, the town still slept, unaware that a man who had once belonged to it was charting a return.

Not to the town, exactly. To her.

He spoke with her last night. Walked with her. Heard her voice break into that familiar cadence only she had ever carried. It hadn't been much, five minutes, perhaps less, but it had been enough.

She was not indifferent.

But she was engaged.

Rodney Wilkinson had stood at her side, publicly confident, privately watchful.

He'd brushed her arm and leaned close when she laughed at someone else's joke. Not with affection but with ownership. A silent assertion of place. Quinton hadn't intervened. But that touch, more than anything, had stayed with him through the night. Nor had he missed the way Rodney angled his body, the way his eyes tracked every word. He wasn't a man in love. He was a man in possession. And somehow, his hands had always been too clean.

Quinton wasn't sure which was worse.

Still, Mary-Ann had chosen to walk with him. That mattered.

He wouldn't plead. He wouldn't press. She was not a prize to be won, and he would not dishonor her or himself by trying to pull her away through force or desperation.

But he *would* remind her.

Not just of what they'd shared but of who she was when she was with him.

There was a difference.

She had laughed, once, with a kind of freedom he hadn't seen in her eyes the night before. And though her smile at dinner had been careful, it had cracked, just once, when she met his gaze.

That was where he'd begin.

Not with letters. Not with declarations. But with the small things. A shared memory. A well-timed observation. A burning question about the docks, the ledgers, and the shipping practices that had always sparked her curiosity.

He would approach as an ally. Let her remember what it was to be known.

And if she asked why he had come back, not to town, but to *her,* he would answer simply: Because you were the part of my life I never meant to leave behind. He remembered the last days and how silence pressed against his skin like stone, how the absence of her voice felt more suffocating than darkness. He held on to phrases she'd once said, replayed them like prayers. Not to escape. To remain human. And when the door finally opened, it wasn't light that struck him first. It was the cold. And the realization that he had lived, barely, without her.

A soft knock at the door pulled him from his thoughts.

Kenworth stepped in with practiced ease, a folded waistcoat over one arm and a knowing smirk at the ready. He glanced at Quinton's half-dressed state with theatrical concern. "Forgive the interruption, my lord, but if you mean to conquer hearts or shipping conspiracies today, might I suggest trousers?"

Quinton turned from the window, one brow lifting as the

corners of his mouth edged into something dangerously close to amusement. "And here I thought bare resolve would suffice."

Kenworth gave a prim bow, his expression painfully neutral. "The Brigade might allow it. Society, I fear, would not. Though I suspect Miss Seaton might tolerate a bit more than most."

Quinton smiled, a real one this time. Steady. Focused.

He moved to the dressing stand, running a hand over the folded waistcoat before pulling it on with practiced ease. The jacket followed, then the cravat, looser than regulation but enough. He adjusted the cuffs, straightened the hem, and caught a glimpse of himself in the mirror. Still lean. Still standing. No medals now. No burden. Just purpose.

"Trousers, then." Kenworth nodded and turned for the door. As he exited, his voice drifted back without turning: "I'll leave the war plans out, just in case."

He dressed with purpose, each button a choice, and each layer was armor for the day ahead. He would start at the docks. Quiet questions. Familiar routes.

Barrington had mentioned a name two nights ago, Percival Trent, a clerk in the Home Office with a reputation for precision and discretion. Not loud, not flashy. But well-placed. He'd signed off on several redirected reports, and Wilkinson, it seemed, had once answered to him. It might be nothing. Or it might be a place to start.

Let her see him not as the man who had vanished but as the one who had come back, changed, yes, but still hers. He didn't know what she would choose. But he knew what he'd fight for: not the past they'd lost, but the future she still carried in her hands. If she truly remembered him, then the rest would follow.

Chapter Fifteen

THAT SAME THURSDAY, past the noonday heat, the pace of the day slowed to a measured beat. The docks smelled of rope, brine, and the sour tang of pitch. Quinton moved with quiet purpose, his boots tapping over damp planks as the morning sun climbed pale over the harbor. Salt hung sharp in the air, mingling with the scent of soaked wood, the kind that seeped into clothing and lingered there. Mist clung low to the waterline, blurring the outlines of ships and softening the world into hush. He drew it in slowly, steadying himself.

There was something about the light at this hour. It was cool, honest, and unrelenting. It didn't comfort. It revealed.

Crews were only just beginning to stir. Voices drifted across the moored ships, threaded through the creak of timber and the sharp clang of a dropped chain.

He paused near a stack of crates labeled for *Montrose & Co.*, scanning the activity. The rhythm of the port hadn't changed. But something beneath it had. A ship he once knew, *The Redwake*, sat moored in the far berth, sails furled like resting wings. He didn't recognize the crew. A younger man stood where Old Thatch used to smoke his pipe, and the deck boards had been replaced. They were newer and brighter but stripped of memory. He could feel it, the way certain men fell quiet when he passed, how foremen stood a little straighter, how glances darted and turned away too quickly.

Barrington had mentioned a name: Lyle Merton. A dockhand,

formerly under Wilkinson's clerk, now worked odd hours and showed up on manifests without clear assignments. Quinton had marked the name and the habit. Men didn't wander into extra labor without a reason, not when hours were tallied with precision and pay was tight.

He spotted a figure near the edge of the quay, sorting lengths of rope into loops far too tidy for the hour. Broad-shouldered, close-cropped hair, a faded blue cap.

Quinton approached slowly, keeping his hands visible and his voice low. "Merton?"

The man glanced up. "Aye."

"Captain Hollingsworth," she said evenly "Just quiet inquiries today."

Merton looked him over, then returned to his ropes. His hands moved more slowly now, the loops less precise. He didn't meet Quinton's gaze. There was wariness in the tightness of his jaw, the careful way he chose each motion as if he were buying himself time. "Ain't much to say."

"You worked under a man named Crowley?"

A pause. Just long enough.

"For a bit. He left."

"And Wilkinson?"

Another pause. The rope slipped slightly in his grip. "Still around. Big plans."

Quinton raised a brow. "Barrington said he rarely shows his face down here."

Merton shrugged. "Now and then. Mostly keeps to the ledgers. Not much use for wet boots."

Quinton let the silence stretch, then nodded once and stepped back. "Thank you."

As he turned to go, Merton added, almost too quietly: "Some things don't get written down, sir."

Quinton didn't reply, but the words stuck. It was the kind of thing a man only said when the truth was more dangerous than silence. Quinton didn't press. Not here. Not with eyes watching and boots echoing off wet planks. But the knot behind his ribs tightened. This wasn't misfiled cargo or ledger mistakes. This was something people were afraid of. Something someone had worked hard to bury.

⇛⇜

MARY-ANN LIFTED THE lid on a tin of oat biscuits and peered inside with something close to dread.

Empty.

Bainbridge's arrival had been sudden and, as always, noisy. The front door had barely shut before her voice filled the hall, followed by the unmistakable rustle of paper patterns, clinking buttons in a tin, and an exasperated rustle of fabric that sounded like a battle standard being unfurled. She now occupied the best chair by the fire, arms draped in swaths of ivory and pale green fabric.

"It's a disaster," Bainbridge said mournfully. "I wanted the green for the ribbons, not the sleeves. And now I have a dozen yards of the wrong fabric, and none of the right, and the modiste insists I agreed to this shade, *this shade*, Mary. Look at it. It's like over-steeped tea."

Mary-Ann set the tin down and leaned against the sideboard, a smile tugging at the edge of her mouth despite the hollowness still lingering in her chest.

"Can't you repurpose it for bows? Or table runners?"

Bainbridge sighed. "Perhaps. If I don't burn it first."

She tossed one bolt of fabric onto the settee and reached for her tea. "You're distracted."

Mary-Ann blinked. "Am I?"

"You haven't said a word about my dramatic reversal of fortune. Usually, you at least pretend to be impressed."

Mary-Ann smoothed the fabric between her fingers, watching the way the light caught the dull sheen. "I'm sorry. I didn't sleep well."

Bainbridge studied her for a moment. "Is it about last night?"

A silence hung between them, delicate and full.

"It's nothing," Mary-Ann said quickly. "I'm just… tired."

"Hmm," Bainbridge replied, utterly unconvinced. "Is it the man who watches you too closely, or the one who's never looked away?"

Mary-Ann gave her a look. A slow blink. A half-turn toward the window. She didn't speak, but her hand rose to rub her temple absently, as if to ward off something.

"You think I don't notice things," Bainbridge said airily. "But I've planned an entire wedding with Barrington. I can read tension better than I read measurements."

Mary-Ann laughed, and it startled her. A true laugh. Not forced, not polite.

"There she is," Bainbridge said softly. "I was starting to worry."

Mary-Ann looked down at the fabric again.

"You can't say yes to something just because it looks good on paper," Bainbridge added. "You'll regret it."

Mary-Ann froze. She hadn't meant to, but her fingers clenched. The line struck too close. She tried to shake it off, but Bainbridge's words lingered like a thread caught on a splinter. It wasn't just the dress. It was everything lately. Rodney's sudden attentiveness, her father's trust in him, and the silence around Quinton that echoed far too loud. Rodney always said the right things. Always made sense on paper. And wasn't that the trouble?

"The dress, I mean," Bainbridge said too quickly.

"Of course."

QUINTON MADE HIS way back from the harbor on foot, his hands in his coat pockets, thoughts churning in rhythm with the steady beat of his boots on the stone. Merton's words stayed with him. *Some things don't get written down.* That could mean anything or everything.

He passed the grocer, nodded at a man stacking apples, and turned onto the lane that curved toward the green. The breeze carried the scent of salt and hearth smoke, and the church bells began to chime the hour.

He wasn't sure if he meant to see her today. Not yet. Not like this. But the thought of her, retreating behind that careful smile, folding herself back into safe expectations, was enough to keep him walking.

Just a little farther. Maybe he'd pass her street. Maybe that was all.

He slowed at the next corner, his boots scuffing against uneven cobblestones. A glance, just a glance, toward the familiar row of houses. He told himself it was a coincidence that his feet simply knew the way. But his heart beat faster all the same.

And maybe it wouldn't be. Maybe it would be the beginning of something he hadn't dared let himself hope for. One more corner. One more pause. He wasn't sure what he hoped to see: a curtain drawn back, a flash of movement, a shadow near the glass. Anything to suggest she was thinking of him too. But even if she wasn't at the window, he could still believe she might be near it. Reading. Waiting. Wondering. And that was enough for now.

MARY-ANN STOOD AT the window after Mrs. Bainbridge left, watching the lane below. The light had shifted. Shadows from the trees outside spilled across the floor like slow-moving tides. She touched the windowpane, cool beneath her fingertips, and closed her eyes just long enough to remember the sound of Quinton's voice the night before. Low. Certain. Too real to forget.

She opened her eyes again. The street was still, but she stared a moment longer, half-expecting to see the edge of a coat or the flicker of a familiar silhouette. The thought unsettled her and rooted her to the place.

The fabric still draped the settee. A biscuit tin sat open beside her untouched tea. She had been still too long.

She could almost feel the tug beneath her ribs, that sharp, familiar flicker of unrest that meant she'd nearly made a decision. The room was too quiet now. Even the wind had stilled as if waiting. She pressed her fingers against the folded paper again. Not just a warning. A map. Not just suspicion. Intention. She didn't know where it would lead. However, standing still wouldn't answer anything.

She folded the note and slipped it into her reticule. The words lived there now, tucked against her side, whispering between each breath.

Don't trust the man with clean hands.

There was so much she didn't know. But she wasn't ready to stand still either. She turned from the window, but not away from the question.

Chapter Sixteen

FRIDAY, JUST AFTER sunrise, a fresh glow painted the horizon with hope. Mary-Ann had risen early, the house still and dim, and paced from room to room like a ghost uncertain of its purpose. The parlor, the study, even the morning room. Everything was too quiet, too contained. She'd picked up the shawl from the hook by the door without thought and stepped outside.

The wind had picked up by the time Mary-Ann reached the edge of the green. She hadn't meant to walk so far. She hadn't meant to leave the house at all. But the walls had begun to feel too close, and the air inside too still. The trees here bent gently in the breeze, their leaves whispering above her like voices she almost remembered.

She didn't plan a direction. Her feet simply knew the path. Past the green, along the winding walk lined with sea grass and stone, until the cliffs emerged just beyond the hedgerow. From there, the whole of the North Sea stretched wide and blue gray under a sky still deciding whether it meant to clear. The breeze off the water met her like an old friend. It was cool, honest, and bracing.

Her mind wandered, unspooling thoughts she'd spent months trying to suppress, her feelings, as she tried to make peace with losing him. She told herself a hundred times that he was gone, that grief would settle like dust if she only waited long enough. And yet when she saw him again, standing whole and alive, it hadn't felt like resurrection. It had felt like the truth returning. The lie had been every day without him.

And now he was here. Breathing the same salt wind. Watching her. And she didn't know whether to run from him or collapse into the space between them.

She stood alone on the path, her shawl pulled tight around her shoulders, staring out over the low stone wall toward where the sea would be. Professor Tresham once said the sea made better listeners than people. She hadn't understood what he meant until now. She had seen it earlier, wide and endless, but from here, it was hidden behind the slope and trees. Still, she could feel it in the wind, in the hush between leaves. It was never far. Not really.

She turned to head back and nearly collided with him.

Quinton.

He stopped just short, hands raised instinctively. "Forgive me. I didn't see—"

"No," she said quickly. "It's all right. I wasn't watching."

They stood there, not quite close enough to touch. Not quite ready to move away.

The wind stirred again, brushing hair across her cheek. She tucked it behind her ear with fingers that felt clumsy.

"You walk early," she said.

"Sometimes."

He looked as he had the night of the charity dinner. Sharply dressed, with a hint of tiredness around the eyes. But now he wasn't surrounded by noise and candlelight. Now he was just a man standing in the morning, watching her as if she were the only thing in the world not blurred by wind and distance.

"I went to the docks," he said.

She nodded. "And?"

"There's something wrong. The more I ask, the less anyone seems willing to say."

She met his eyes then. "I believe you."

He didn't expect that, not so easily, not so openly. A dozen half-formed arguments caught in his throat, all of them rendered useless by the certainty in her gaze. He studied her face, looking for doubt, for hesitation, but there was none. Only weariness, and something that looked a little too much like hope.

"You always did see things clearly," he said. "Even when no one else wanted to look."

She exhaled, slowly and quietly. "It's harder now. Everything feels murky. But I remember how things used to be, how my uncle handled the manifests. How certain ships arrived with more cargo than they had when they left. I think something started changing even before you left."

It should have been a relief. It wasn't. Not quite. The silence between them filled again, not with tension, but with something heavier. Familiar.

"Mary-Ann…"

He took one step closer. She didn't move.

"I never stopped—"

"Don't," she said softly. "Please."

His breath caught. Not at her words, but the way she said them. It hurt to ask him to stop, like it would hurt more if he didn't.

He reached for her hand. Slowly. He gave her time to pull away. She didn't. Their breath mingled in the space between them, suspended, neither of them willing to be the first to break it.

He searched her face not for permission but for recognition. And what he saw there stopped him. She didn't flinch or look away. She held his gaze like a mooring line as if she were anchoring herself to this one moment. There were no more questions in her eyes. Just a quiet challenge and something softer beneath it. Recognition.

Their fingers met, tentative at first. Then sure. For the smallest moment, she remembered a spring morning two years ago when he'd tried to teach her a sailor's knot. She had failed miserably and blamed the breeze for his poor technique. Later, still laughing as they stepped inside, she knocked over an inkwell on the writing desk and ruined her dress. He'd offered to replace it but instead brought her a tin of lemon drops. "Far more practical," he'd said, deadpan as if it were a matter of naval policy. The memory struck her now, sudden and unguarded, and she laughed, just once, under her breath. He smiled in response, and the tension shifted into something warmer. Braver. His thumb brushed the edge of her glove, and that was all it took.

He leaned in. She did too.

Their lips met in the space between restraint and longing, shattering every careful silence they'd built. The kiss wasn't perfect. It wasn't rehearsed. It was raw and aching and full of all the years they'd spent trying to forget how this felt.

She pressed closer, her hand finding his coat lapel. He gathered her in, as if he couldn't help it, as if he'd spent three years with this absence carved into his chest.

When they pulled apart, neither of them spoke. Mary-Ann's heart was thudding so hard she could feel it in her fingertips. Her lips still tingled, not only from the kiss, but from the truth of it. The unspoken ache, the certainty that neither time nor distance had dulled whatever invisible thread still held them fast.

Her breath trembled against his collar.

He touched her cheek with the back of his hand, reverently. It wasn't a goodbye, not quite. But it wasn't a promise either. Just a moment that held still, fragile, and was too real to put into words.

"I'm not sorry that happened," he said, voice low but steady. It was all he gave her, and everything she would remember.

She could have answered. Should have. But the truth was still too large, too bright to speak aloud. It pulsed behind her ribs like a secret she'd never meant to give away. He didn't press her. He didn't need to. Her silence told him everything louder, deeper, more honestly than words ever could.

Without a word, he took a step back.

She let him go. She didn't trust herself to speak. Her throat was tight, her thoughts unraveled. If she opened her mouth, she wasn't sure what might fall out. Would it be something foolish, something brave, something true?

But her eyes never left his.

Neither of them looked away.

He walked away first, slow and sure, as though putting distance between them required more effort than he'd admit. Mary-Ann stayed where she was, watching as his back receded down the path. Her hands were still folded at her waist, but her fingers trembled faintly against the fabric of her glove.

When she finally turned, the wind caught her shawl again. She didn't fix it. Let it flutter. Let it pull. Because some part of her still stood in the moment they had shared, anchored there, breathless and undone.

She walked slowly, each step with a strange mix of lightness and ache. The path felt different now, as though it remembered what had just happened. The wind had gentled, or maybe she'd simply stopped noticing its bite. Her hand drifted once to her lips, then dropped quickly, as if the memory could be disturbed by touching it too often.

She didn't try to name what the kiss meant. Not yet. But it lived in her now in the racing of her pulse, in the quiet sense that something had shifted. Not broken. Not healed. Just changed.

She passed the corner where Mrs. Haversham always placed her flowerpots, still damp from the morning watering. A cat lounged on a windowsill across the street, watching her as if privy to secrets best kept silent. A boy darted from a doorway with a kite trailing behind him, laughing as the fabric snapped in the breeze. Nothing looked different. And yet every breath felt strange in her chest, fuller, harder to hold.

The town was waking up around her, the soft murmur of brooms against stone, the squeak of a window being opened. Life continuing. But she walked through it as though wrapped in another hour entirely. One that still echoed with his voice, his touch, his kiss.

And though the town still lay quiet ahead, the day no different than any other, she knew something had begun, something she couldn't undo and didn't want to. Not ever.

Chapter Seventeen

SATURDAY MORNING, WITH mist lingering along the rooftops, Mary-Ann's mind refused to stay in the present. She sat at the breakfast table, the scent of tea mingling with sea air that slipped through a cracked window. She hadn't touched her toast. The Sommer Sentinel lay open beside her, though her gaze drifted more to the sea beyond the pane than to the ink on the page.

Her father turned a page with a dry rustle. "This is a report on the latest information about those two children rescued after hunting dragons in the beach caves," he said, amused. "Wooden swords and all. They were looking for treasure, it seems. Got themselves caught by the tide."

Mary-Ann blinked, then glanced down at the column.

She hadn't thought of the beach caves in years. As a girl, she'd once begged Hamish to take her exploring. He had come, of course, armed with nothing but a walking stick he called a 'sword' and a pouch of peppermints. They hadn't found dragons or treasure, only a flock of startled gulls and an old fisherman's net. But she remembered how the cave walls had shimmered faintly with dampness, and how the tide whispered secrets as it crept in.

She frowned now, unsettled by how quickly that memory had surfaced. It was just a children's story, a harmless adventure. But something about the image of those two boys with wooden swords felt like a thread left dangling. And the tide, always the tide, never waited long.

"Two Rescued After Seaside Dragon Hunt"

Two children were rescued last week after becoming trapped by the tide inside one of the shallow beach caves north of Sommer-by-the-Sea. According to their mother, the children entered the cave with wooden swords and a tin lantern "in search of drag-ons and buried treasure." Neither was injured, though both were soaked and tearful by the time a local fisherman helped pull them free. The Town Council reminds residents to be mind-ful of the tides and not to enter coastal formations without an adult present.

"They're lucky they didn't drown," her father muttered, shaking his head. "Foolish thing to do."

Mary-Ann nodded faintly, but her thoughts were elsewhere.

She folded the paper and set it aside. The kiss lingered like warmth on her skin, impossible to ignore. She hadn't meant to think of it, not now, not with her father seated across from her. But it returned anyway. Quinton's hand at her back, the press of his mouth against hers, the way time had slipped sideways for one breathless instant.

"Rodney stopped by the office again yesterday," her father said, dabbing his mouth with a napkin. "Went over the shipment receipts from last quarter. He took quite an interest in the reweigh totals. Thought they were off."

Mary-Ann's spine straightened. "Rodney?"

"Mm," her father said, pouring another cup of coffee. "Smart man, that one. He reminds me of your uncle in his younger years. Curious about the right things."

She managed a smile, but it felt thin. "Has he been helping with the books long?"

"Oh, on and off," her father said. "Only when he asks. I've given him leave to familiarize himself with the business. Once you're married, it'll be part his, too."

He took another sip of coffee, then added, "In fact, it might be a good time for you to step back from the ledgers and the office work." Rodney mentioned you've been looking a touch worn. He says you're always scribbling in margins, always with ink on your hands."

Mary-Ann blinked. "Did he."

Her father chuckled, clearly amused. "He meant it kindly. You'll have other duties soon enough. The wife of Rodney Wilkinson will be managing invitations and estates, not shipping weights and dock figures. You've done your share already. No one could say otherwise."

Mary-Ann looked down at her toast. She wasn't hungry. Not for food. Not for assumptions disguised as certainties. The toast had gone cold. Her fingers brushed her palm absently, and she noticed a faint trace of ink smudged near her thumb, left from her notes the night before, no doubt. She rubbed it with her napkin, but the mark only faded. It didn't disappear. Like the life she'd built, it clung. She wasn't ashamed of it. She had never been. But suddenly, she saw it for what it was: the thing Rodney wanted erased.

She remembered the first time Rodney had offered to help with the books. He'd come into the office with a bouquet of roses and a quick smile, claiming he wanted to understand her world. She'd welcomed the gesture then. She was even grateful for his interest. But what followed hadn't been help. It had been an oversight. He'd asked questions, yes, but offered unsolicited advice just as quickly. One afternoon, he'd reached for her ledger with a freshly gloved hand and laughed when she pulled it back. "Careful, love," he'd said. "You'll get ink on the upholstery."

At the time, she'd forced a laugh and let the moment pass. But it came back to her now, sharp and unwelcome.

She excused herself quietly, pressing a kiss to her father's cheek before retreating from the room. But as she reached the door, she hesitated. Her father had once sat with her at this same table, guiding her through invoices and balance sheets, explaining how to double-check reweigh records and where to look for losses. She had earned his trust through diligence, not inheritance.

And yet here he sat, handing the reins to someone else. Not because he no longer believed in her but because he no longer saw her. Not fully. She wondered if he noticed how little she came to the office these days. Or how often Rodney spoke for her without asking.

She glanced back once. He was buttering another slice of toast, humming softly under his breath. Content. Unworried. It was the most ordinary thing in the world, and it made her chest ache.

Her footsteps echoed too crisply against the floorboards. Upstairs, in the quiet of her room, she unpinned her hair with trembling fingers and crossed to the window seat. The view stretched out toward the sea, distant and still. A glint of sun touched the water, indifferent to the ache behind her ribs.

The kiss was still with her. Not just the sensation but the meaning. It hadn't been a mistake. And yet, her father's voice echoed in her mind, "Once you're married, it'll be part his, too." The words sat like a stone in her chest. Rodney was not unkind. He was clever and capable. But the way her father spoke, it was as if her life were already sorted into ledgers and forecasts, promises drafted on her behalf.

And Quinton… he hadn't asked for promises. He hadn't asked for anything. He had simply stood there, steady and sure, and kissed her as if it were the only truth they had left.

Her gaze drifted to the wall just beside her wardrobe. Slowly, she rose, crossed the room, and knelt before the small seam in the wainscoting. Her fingers found the loosened panel easily now. Behind it, the booklet waited, its cloth cover frayed and colorless in the dim morning light. She hesitated for a breath. The first time she'd found it, she'd nearly dismissed it as just another forgotten receipt log. It wasn't until she noticed the unfamiliar hand and the strange notations that she realized this wasn't meant for anyone else's eyes.

The cloth was rough beneath her fingers, worn soft at the corners like an old handkerchief. She pulled it out and returned to the window seat, placing the worn folio across her knees like a secret only she had earned the right to carry. The booklet felt heavier today. As though it knew it was being seen differently.

She opened to the torn message, her thumb brushing lightly over the faded ink. The edges were still jagged, as though whatever truth it carried had been yanked out too quickly.

Don't trust the man with clean hands.

Each time she read it, the words took on a new shape. Today, they echoed differently because Rodney had always had clean hands. Immaculate boots. A pristine cravat. And now he was reviewing shipments. Alone. Without her knowledge.

She turned the paper over as if the back might suddenly yield more. But there was nothing. Just the pulse behind her temples and the slow, steady realization that she could no longer pretend not to see what she had always been too careful to name.

A knock came at the front door, measured and familiar. Moments later, Hollis's footsteps sounded on the stairs. A quiet rap, then his voice through the door: "A note for you, miss. From Lord Barrington."

She rose to take it, smoothing the paper between her fingers. Hollis bowed slightly before he left, and she returned to the window. The note was folded precisely, its seal intact, and the handwriting firm, clean, unmistakably deliberate, and unmistakably Barrington's. She broke the seal and read the line once, then again, each word sharpening the air around her.

Had Quinton asked him to write it? Or had Barrington acted on his own, sensing her hesitation, her need to be brought into the fold? She didn't know. But she was grateful either way. Barrington, for all his dry reserve and formality, had never looked at her like she didn't belong. And that, today, felt like something close to loyalty.

Mary-Ann folded the note with care. The ache in her chest hadn't eased, but her purpose had sharpened. She crossed to her writing desk, tucked the message into a drawer, and rested her palm briefly on its smooth wooden edge. For a moment, she let herself look at the small drawer beneath where she still kept old manifests and the odd receipt written in Hamish's familiar looping hand. A torn corner of paper peeked out, and she tucked it gently back into place.

Her fingers lingered there. How many hours had she spent here, doing the work no one else bothered with? Sorting figures, deciphering notes, and building the quiet foundation that had kept her father's business from slipping into confusion, especially now that Hamish had passed away? She wasn't a girl with ink-stained hands. She was a woman who had held the seams of a legacy together.

She straightened slowly, her shawl falling back into place across her shoulders. The ache was still there, but she didn't flinch from it. Not now. She crossed to the window once more and let her gaze drift across the town below. From here, it all looked unchanged, chimneys rising, smoke curling, roofs glinting in the sun. But something in her had shifted. She wasn't waiting anymore. Not for her father to see her, not for Rodney to step aside, not even for Quinton to speak first. This was her life. Her family. Her legacy. And she would not be written out of it quietly.

And perhaps she'd ask Mrs. Bainbridge about Professor Tresham's latest visit…

She thought of her mother then, strong-willed, soft-voiced. "Don't ever let anyone marry you out of your name," she'd once said while pinning up her hair. "If you lose your name, you'd better gain something stronger."

Mary-Ann wasn't sure yet what she was gaining. But she knew what she wouldn't surrender.

She crossed to her wardrobe, opened the drawer where she kept her work apron, and set it carefully atop the desk. Not because she needed it, but because she might. She tied her hair back with practiced ease. The tide was shifting. She could feel it. And this time, she wouldn't let it pull her under.

She hadn't asked what Quinton discovered. She wished she

had.

He was looking for something. So was she. Maybe they weren't so far apart after all.

And for the first time, she found herself wondering what Quinton had learned at the docks.

Chapter Eighteen

SUNDAY MORNING, AS storm clouds began their slow dance offshore, the distant tide echoed her inner turmoil. The door to Lord Barrington's townhouse opened with a smooth efficiency that seemed to mirror the man himself. Mary-Ann stepped inside, greeted by the crisp scent of lavender polish and parchment, the hush of carpets softening every sound. The light was soft and diffused, catching the trim of each corniced wall, and the brass door hinges gleamed without a smudge. Even the ticking of the hallway clock seemed to hesitate, muffled beneath the plush runner. She folded Barrington's note again and slipped it into her reticule, the creased paper warm from her palm.

"Welcome back to Sommer Chase, Miss Seaton," Mr. Sanderson, the butler, said, his voice smooth and familiar. She remembered him now, the way he always seemed to anticipate needs before they were spoken.

"This way, Miss Seaton."

She followed, her gloves tucked neatly in one hand, her shawl knotted with deliberate care. The townhouse was handsome but not ostentatious. Dark wood, narrow hall tables, the occasional gleam of silver. it felt like a place where things were done quietly but thoroughly, just like the man who owned it.

They reached a receiving room framed with high windows and lined shelves. The butler gestured toward a settee, then disappeared without a sound. Mary-Ann remained standing for a moment, her gaze sweeping the quiet space. She recognized the clean order of the room, the kind where decisions were made, and secrets were stored. This wasn't the kind of parlor where women were expected to sit and embroider politely. She had once sat in such rooms beside her mother, listening to conversations she wasn't meant to understand. This was different. She wasn't here to listen. She was here to speak.

Her eyes trailed along the bookshelves. There were treatises, reports, and a brass compass resting on a leather-bound logbook. This wasn't a gentleman's idle library. This was a room of function, not ornament.

Somewhere down the corridor, a door clicked open, and the faintest ripple of voices echoed, a light female voice, followed by a deeper one she didn't recognize. Mrs. Bainbridge, perhaps. There was a laugh, then a muttered exclamation about guest lists. Mary-Ann allowed herself the smallest smile. Mrs. Bainbridge, it seemed, was still fending off wedding mayhem.

She wished, briefly, that she could ask Mrs. Bainbridge what Quinton had discovered at the docks, what she thought of it, what Barrington thought of it. But this visit was not about wishes. It was about facts.

She turned toward the window, letting the soft light calm her nerves. The folio remained hidden behind the wainscoting at home. She had brought nothing with her, not yet. But a name lingered on her tongue. A ship name. One that had appeared more than once in the booklet's tight scrawl.

The Redwake.

Before she could second-guess herself, the door opened.

"Miss Seaton."

Lord Barrington entered with his usual composed precision. He wore no medals, no ceremonial cravat, just a well-cut coat, waistcoat, and the expression of a man who preferred clarity over charm.

"I appreciate you coming," he said, gesturing to a chair across from his desk.

Mary-Ann dipped her head slightly, then sat.

"You said this concerned a matter Quinton raised."

"It does." Barrington poured her a cup of tea, then his own. "Though he's not the only one who's noticed certain…irregularities."

She lifted her brows. "Irregularities?"

"Letters lost. Receipts misplaced. Crates that left the yard properly marked and weighed but arrived without record. It's subtle. Carefully done. But there's a pattern."

Mary-Ann wrapped her hands around her teacup. "And Quinton saw this at the docks?"

Barrington gave a brief nod. "He followed a discrepancy backward. Quietly. He said he remembered your ledgers always being more precise than the daybooks he reviewed. That your notations flagged inconsistencies the foremen tended to miss."

A flicker of warmth passed through her, unexpected and deeply personal. She wondered if Quinton had really remembered her notes or if Barrington had embellished them for the sake of trust. But the sentiment stayed with her, small and steady. Once, she had combed through ledgers by candlelight while others slept, driven by instinct and precision. And now, those hours were no longer just duty. They were proof.

"I'd like to show you something," Barrington said, rising.

He crossed to a cabinet and returned with a slim stack of folios. "I've had my man make copies of a few manifests from the past three months. All are connected to the same shipping lane. Northbound. All with unverified cargo adjustments."

Mary-Ann scanned the headers. Dates. Ship names. Ports. Her gaze caught a name.

The Redwake.

Barrington noticed. "That one came up twice. Do you recognize it?"

She set the folio down with care. "It's a ship that appears in my father's logs. More than once. And…" she hesitated, then steadied her voice. "I've seen it mentioned elsewhere."

Barrington gave a thoughtful nod, then added, almost absently, "Colonel Rathbone flagged it last quarter. I thought it was odd that Redwake had no escort listed. He's meticulous, that one, old school Ordnance, but reliable."

Mary-Ann absorbed the name without pause. It meant nothing to her yet.

"I can do better," she said quietly. "I've already started."

Barrington gave a satisfied nod and stepped away to retrieve a report from the adjoining room.

The moment he left, the door clicked again.

The sound stirred something in her chest, anticipation, maybe, or a memory still warm from yesterday.

Quinton stood just inside as if he had paused mid-step. His gaze found her instantly. His coat was dusty from the road, his posture a touch weary, but there was nothing uncertain in the way he looked at her. There was no smile, no clever line. Just that steady, anchoring presence she remembered.

"Miss Seaton," he said, quiet and sure.

"Captain."

He crossed the room with measured steps, stopping a pace away. "I wasn't sure you'd come."

"I wasn't either," she said honestly.

A moment stretched between them filled not with awkwardness but with something unnamed. The air felt sharper for it.

"I wanted to thank you," he said. "For listening. And for not looking away."

"I've done enough of that lately."

He gave a faint nod. "Barrington thought it best you heard things plainly."

"He was right."

She studied him, watching the subtle changes since she'd last seen him. The way he stood, hands loose at his sides instead of crossed. The way his gaze didn't drift, didn't retreat. He wasn't guarding himself, not from her. That quiet she sensed wasn't hesitation. It was the stillness of someone who had been through fire and come out tempered. It was watchfulness.

"You already suspected something, didn't you?" he asked.

Mary-Ann hesitated, then answered with the truth. "I had reason to wonder."

"Are you going to tell me what that reason is?"

She met his gaze evenly. "Not yet."

A flicker of something passed over his face. It wasn't offense but understanding. "Then I won't ask. When you are ready to tell me, I'll listen."

She looked down at the folio. "But I can help. I know the rhythms of those ships. And I know when something has been moved just enough to make it look like nothing at all."

"I believe you," he said simply.

He glanced toward the door where Barrington had gone, then back at her. "You're the only one I trust to give us the correct answers." His voice was low but certain, and there was no flattery in it, just fact. It steadied her more than she expected.

Rising with quiet purpose, Mary-Ann smoothed her skirts and moved toward the window.

The sea beyond was barely visible, but she imagined it just the same, restless, waiting.

Barrington returned a moment later with a new set of documents. He spread them across the table.

As Mary-Ann stepped closer, her eyes caught on a peculiar stamp in the corner of one page, a raven with its wings spread wide over a sharp-edged diamond. The ink was faded, almost smudged into the grain of the paper, as if someone had tried to press too lightly. Her stomach turned. Not from fear, exactly, but from the awful clarity that came with recognition. This wasn't a merchant's flourish or a dockhand's stamp. It was deliberate. Delicate in its precision. And wrong. The kind of wrong that wasn't meant to be noticed until it was too late.

A flicker of memory stirred—one corner of the booklet, the ink bled faintly, the shape imperfect but unmistakable. She'd thought it a bird then, but now she knew. It had always been a raven.

Her breath caught. She had seen that same mark before, buried among the strange symbols on the back pages of the hidden booklet. She didn't speak, didn't let her fingers pause too long. But the image stayed fixed in her mind, stark as a warning.

Barrington's eyes flicked up at her, sharp for just a second. Then he nodded, slowly. "You notice details most don't."

"What is that?" she asked lightly, tapping the symbol with one gloved finger. Her tone was casual, even curious.

Barrington followed her gesture and frowned faintly. "Just a yard stamp, I'm sure. Likely from a northern office. They've been using odd symbols lately."

A small nod concealed the quickening pulse at her throat. She didn't correct him. She didn't say she'd seen it before.

As Barrington returned to his desk, she stepped back slightly, pretending to review another page. But her mind stayed on the symbol. It felt like standing at the edge of a shadow, not fully inside it, but aware now that it existed. And that it might be watching back.

Her steps carried her to the table, slow and steady, her gaze catching on the edge of a map half-unrolled across the surface. Her fingers brushed a familiar port name, Berwick, and a flicker of memory stirred. Her father had once shown her how to trace a route with just a compass and a thumb. She had forgotten that until now. It was a quiet thing, but grounding. Like drawing a line between what was and what would be.

Mary-Ann stepped forward, her voice calm and clear.

"Show me where it began."

Chapter Nineteen

MONDAY MORNING BROKE under grey skies, the morning light pressing coolly against the curtains as Mary-Ann awoke uneasy and unrested. The Seaton house was still. Mary-Ann paused at her door, listening for the creak of floorboards or the distant echo of servants' steps. Nothing. Silence wrapped around her like a shawl she'd worn too many nights, waiting for the world to make sense again. She crossed to the desk beneath her bedroom window, her bare feet whispering against the rug. The latch on the wainscoting gave a familiar click, and she reached into the narrow cavity behind it. Her fingers brushed cloth and paper. The booklet was just where she'd left it.

She carried it to the desk and lit a small lamp, shielding the flame with her hand until it caught. Shadows stretched long across the floor, pooling near the corners of the room. She opened the booklet slowly, reverently, as if it were something sacred or cursed. The pages gave a dry rustle, the ink still sharp where it hadn't faded.

Her fingertips traced the familiar marks, Hamish's handwriting, she still believed, or perhaps someone just as practiced. Triangles, dots, slashes. She remembered seeing those in the margins weeks ago and thinking they were some kind of shorthand. But now her gaze moved with purpose.

She turned page after page until she found it, the raven, wings outstretched over a diamond, inked in fine black lines. It was smaller here than on the manifest Barrington had shown her and almost hidden among the other markings. But it was unmistakable.

She turned another page. There it was again. And again. Not next to every entry, but beside certain names and certain routes. Some repeated. Some she recognized from her father's logs. One she remembered because she'd questioned the cargo manifest at the time, a crate marked textiles that had felt too heavy when it was lifted. Her stomach dropped, a slow unraveling of certainty replaced by something colder. She pressed her palm to the page as if touch could make sense of it. The symbol wasn't just a mark. It was a warning. Or a signature. And it was threaded through these pages like a warning no one was meant to follow. What had felt like patterns now looked like purpose. Deliberate. Repeated. Dangerous. Her breath quickened as she leaned closer, heart knocking against her ribs. What if someone knew she was reading this? What if they'd left the booklet to be found? Or worse, to trap whoever did?

This wasn't just a ledger. It was a trail.

She worked in silence, marking the entries with a strip of ribbon as she searched for patterns. The ships weren't all the same, but the destinations were close. Northbound. Rural. One bound for Berwick. Another for a place she'd only seen in letters.

A knock sounded faintly downstairs. She stilled. But after a moment, the silence returned. Only the wind scratched softly at the windowpanes.

She exhaled and leaned back, staring at the booklet.

If this symbol meant what she feared, then Barrington's answer wasn't just inadequate. It was wrong. Or worse. It was deliberate.

And if it was deliberate, then someone had decided she didn't need the truth.

She thought, briefly, of Quinton's voice beside her, the way he used to read figures aloud in a murmur only she could hear. She missed the ease between them. Not just the warmth, but the precision. The way they fit. It wasn't just her heart she trusted him with. It was her mind.

She copied the entries down, exact and careful, onto a fresh sheet of paper, tucking the page into her bodice. She thought, briefly, of taking it straight to Quinton. He would know what to do. He would look at her not as someone fragile or foolish but as a partner. But then she thought of his eyes, shadowed at the edges even when he smiled. In the quiet way he carried his pain, tucked beneath steady words and silence. He had survived something terrible, and she had already lost him once. If there was danger ahead, she could not bear to be the one who led it to his door. Not yet. Not until she was certain it mattered. Not until she knew he was ready.

Before she put the booklet away, she opened the drawer beneath her desk and drew out her private ledger, the one where she'd recorded the weight discrepancies. Leafing through it to the marked pages, she glanced over her notes, one column at a time. Her breath caught. Three of the ships with the raven symbol matched entries she'd flagged weeks ago. The weight differences had seemed small at the time, barely enough to raise concern. But now they weren't anomalies. They were signs. Whoever had kept the booklet had noticed the same things she had and marked them for a reason. When she was finished, she closed the booklet and returned it to the hidden space behind the wainscoting, checking the latch twice.

Only then did she sit back, hands folded over the fabric covering her ribs, and whisper to herself, "You trusted me to find the truth. I hope you still will when I bring it to you."

ELSEWHERE IN SOMMER Chase, Kenworth lingered just outside the study door, holding a silver tray in his hand and wearing a perfectly unimpressed expression on his face. The tray held a single letter, sealed in cream wax, and a small wedge of lemon cake, uneaten, but not unappreciated.

He cleared his throat once. Loudly. Then twice, in case the first had been missed. When no one answered, he shifted the tray to one hand and tapped lightly at the doorframe. "I realize I'm not the foreign secretary," he murmured, "but I do outrank urgency in matters of refreshment."

The door opened a crack. Barrington's voice came, low and taut. "Kenworth, not now."

"You say that every time," Kenworth replied, stepping in without waiting. "But I recall a certain bullet wound in Salamanca, and I don't remember you turning down lemon cake then."

Barrington sighed, shoulders relaxing ever so slightly. He didn't look up. "That was different."

"You were bleeding then," Kenworth said mildly. "Now you're just brooding."

He placed the tray gently on the side table. "Don't let the boy storm out without a biscuit. It's hard to fight empires on an empty stomach."

Barrington didn't answer, but the tension in the room eased by a thread. Kenworth turned to go, his footsteps soft. "Back in a quarter hour. Try not to start a war before the tea."

⇶⇷

QUINTON DIDN'T KNOCK. He let himself into Barrington's study and closed the door behind him with deliberate finality.

Barrington looked up from the map spread across his desk, one brow arching. "You're late."

He stopped just short of the desk, eyes steady but too still. "You lied."

The words came softly, but they carried finality, like something dropped from a great height.

The air in the room contracted. Barrington's brows lifted higher. "Is that how we're going to begin?"

Quinton stepped forward, his jaw tight. He hadn't come to argue, not truly, but the moment the words left Barrington's mouth, something in him snapped taut, like a canvas yanked by a storm wind. "You told her it was a customs seal."

Barrington straightened slightly in his chair, a flicker of caution passing behind his eyes. "I didn't lie. I simplified."

"You downplayed the mark of the Order of Shadows."

He'd seen that symbol once before, etched into a crate in a shadowed storeroom back when the world still thought him missing. At the time, he hadn't known its meaning. Now he did.

Barrington's expression faltered. A shudder of tension passed through his shoulders before he masked it. "She doesn't know what the Order is."

"She will. And she'll know you didn't trust her with the truth."

"I trusted her with what she needed to hear," Barrington said, pushing back from the desk with the practiced calm of a man used to control. "You saw her face, Quinton. She's brave, but she isn't invulnerable."

"You think I don't know that?" Quinton's voice dropped, low and sharp. He took another step forward, hands fisted at his sides. He'd seen the tension in Mary-Ann's hands when she thought no one was looking. The way she stood straighter when someone questioned her work, as though her spine alone could hold back a rising tide. She was brave. But brave didn't mean unbreakable. "You think I haven't watched what all of this has already cost her?"

Barrington leaned back slowly, one hand curling around the arm of his chair. "She's only just stepping into this. If we overwhelm her—"

"She's already in it," Quinton cut in. "And she deserves to know what she's walking toward, not what we've decided she can handle."

The silence that followed stretched tight. Barrington's gaze dropped for a moment, then lifted. It was steady, heavy with calculation.

He still didn't know who had ordered his silence. But this… this narrowed the list.

"If she puts that symbol to paper," he said quietly, "if she speaks it aloud in the wrong company, she won't just be a daughter or a bookkeeper. She'll be a target."

Quinton didn't answer. The words rose. *How much longer do we keep her in the dark?* But the words caught in his throat before he could speak. His loyalty to Barrington warred with something deeper, older, and more visceral.

He had seen what shadows could do to a man. He would not let them close around her.

Barrington met his gaze evenly. "I want her protected. That hasn't changed." He hesitated, his voice dropping, "And until we know more, you will not speak to her of the Order. That's not a suggestion."

Quinton's jaw flexed. He didn't agree, but he nodded once, sharply.

It was the closest thing to rebellion Barrington would tolerate and the closest thing to obedience Quinton would allow himself.

Quinton's fists slowly unclenched. "Then let me do it properly."

Barrington stood. Walked to a drawer and pulled out the copied manifest Mary-Ann had seen, and held it out. "Then start here."

Quinton took it and studied the familiar notations. If this was the trail Mary-Ann had followed, he needed to know exactly where it led and who had walked it before her. He folded the page and tucked it into his coat. He didn't speak the vow aloud. He didn't have to.

He thought briefly of the wind on the cliffs, the feel of her hand in his, and the way her breath had caught just before she kissed him. That moment lived beneath everything now quiet but constant, like the tide.

A soft knock echoed faintly down the corridor. Then Kenworth's voice: "And do try not to dismantle the government without your waistcoat, my lord."

Barrington returned to his desk without a word. The room became silent once again, but it wasn't peaceful. Quinton paused just outside the door, his hand brushing the inner pocket where the manifest now rested. He should've felt more prepared. Instead, he felt the pressure of everything he hadn't said to her, and everything she had already risked without knowing what lay ahead.

Down the corridor, the scent of bergamot and old paper hung in the air. The house had always been quiet, but this silence carried something heavier. Expectation. Fear. Hope. He thought of Mary-Ann, hunched over a ledger by candlelight, refusing to overlook a single figure. She didn't even know she was brave. She simply was.

He'd lost her once and nearly lost himself in the process. He would not lose her again, not to the Order, not to secrecy, and not to silence.

If she was already in the current, then he'd be the one to face the undertow.

Chapter Twenty

Tuesday morning, with a lingering chill in the air and secrets whispered by the old walls, the day began in quiet determination. *The Redwake* had come into port before dawn, its arrival quiet, its crew even quieter. But Mary-Ann had noticed. She'd seen the name before, inked beside a symbol no one wanted to explain. And still, no one had. Not Barrington. Not Quinton. She had watched them both and read between the lines, what they didn't say. If answers didn't come to her, she would go looking for them herself.

The ship sat low in the water, its hull stained from long use and sea spray, the lettering on its stern faded but still legible. Mary-Ann stood a short distance away, her bonnet tilted just enough to shade her eyes without appearing secretive. She had chosen this ship for one reason only. No one aboard would know her face.

She kept her expression mild, almost aimless, as she strolled closer. The bustle of the docks helped cloak her movement, men calling out cargo counts, gulls shrieking overhead, and the constant creak of wood and rope. She wore a simple walking dress, the kind any woman might wear while delivering a message or collecting a package. A stray strand of hair tickled her cheek, but she didn't brush it away. Any unnecessary movement might draw notice. Her gloves were unadorned. Her curiosity, however, was sharp.

She circled toward a stack of crates near the gangplank, pausing as though checking a tag. A few paces away, a dockworker barked at another man to shift the balance of the load. None of them looked twice at her. That was the advantage, wasn't it? No one questioned a woman with a soft voice and well-stitched gloves.

A manifest was pinned near the cargo ramp, fluttering slightly in the breeze. She stepped forward, adjusted her gloves, and leaned in.

One of the lines caught her eye: a crate bound for Durham, recorded at a weight she knew was false. She'd seen its duplicate listed elsewhere, and that one had been almost half the size. Her pulse quickened. She followed the entries down the page, eyes narrowing. There. Another. This one is bound for a smaller town upriver. It, too, was overweight.

She stepped back, glancing toward the crates. If she could find the one labeled for Durham—

"Careful there, miss."

The voice was close and unfamiliar. She turned as a hand reached toward her shoulder, not roughly, but firm. One of the dockhands, his sleeves rolled high and his face ruddy from the sun.

"This ship isn't for the curious. Best be on your way."

Mary-Ann lifted her chin. I was told that a parcel arrived on this vessel. I only meant to—"

"You don't want to be on this one," he said, his voice lowering. "Some cargo fights back."

It was the kind of thing a man only said when truth was more dangerous than silence.

Her heart gave a single, hard thud.

The man's gaze flicked toward another sailor, and Mary-Ann felt the shift. She had lingered too long.

She stepped back at once, murmured a polite thank-you, and turned down the dock with steady steps. Her spine prickled as she walked as if the air behind her had thickened. Not hurried. Not yet.

Only once she reached the corner past the warehouse did she let out her breath. Her palms were damp inside her gloves. But she had something now. Confirmation. *The Redwake* was part of it. Whatever *it* was.

❯❯❯❮❮❮

THE DOCK BEHIND her faded with every step, but Mary-Ann's mind refused to still. Her heart had steadied, but her thoughts had not. If danger truly lurked behind those crates, and someone had warned her away, it meant she was closer to something real. And she was no longer content with shadows.

She walked along the path edging the cliffs, the sea churning far below. The wind tugged at her shawl, reddening her cheeks, but she didn't mind. Her nerves needed the air.

He stood near the overlook, eyes fixed on the docks far below. From this height, the ships were no more than shadows gliding through water and mist, but he'd seen her. Plain dress. Steady step. Too close to *The Redwake*. He hadn't followed. Not yet.

She hadn't gone far before she saw him.

Quinton.

He stood ahead on the path, half-turned toward the horizon, coat buttons gleaming faintly in the light. He turned before she could call out, as if he'd known she was coming all along. A flicker of surprise crossed her face, disappearing almost as quickly as it had appeared.

Their eyes met, and for a moment, everything between them went still.

"Out walking?" he asked, voice gentle.

"Something like that."

She hadn't meant to see him. And yet, part of her wasn't surprised.

They fell into step easily, the space between them filling with the rhythm of shared silence. It surprised her how natural it felt. Like stepping back into a melody she hadn't realized she remembered. No tug, no resistance, just the ease of someone who saw her as she was. She didn't speak of *The Redwake*. He didn't ask. But the air between them was rich with the things they didn't say.

They used to walk like this most evenings, circling the edge of town with no particular destination in mind. He would ask about her day, and unlike most men, he actually listened. He never hurried her, never spoke over her. The memory surfaced with quiet clarity, softening something in her chest.

"You look well," she said at last.

"I'm getting there."

A pause. Then a small smile tugged at her lips. "You were always good at returning from impossible places."

"And you," he said quietly, "were always the one I wanted to return to."

She looked at him sharply, her heart stuttering, but his gaze had shifted back to the sea.

They stopped near the overlook, the sea roaring below.

He reached for her hand but didn't quite take it. Instead, his fingers brushed hers. He hesitated, his mouth parting slightly as if to say more. But then his jaw tightened, and he glanced away.

"Be careful, Mary-Ann," he said. "Especially now."

She wanted to ask what he meant and question him until the truth spilled out. But the look in his eyes stopped her. It wasn't fear. It was guilt. And that, somehow, unsettled her more.

Her breath caught. In that brief contact, she felt steadied. The storm of the morning, the doubt of the docks, none of it reached her here.

There was more. She could see it, feel it, in the tension at the corners of his mouth. But he said nothing else, and she didn't press him. Not yet.

It was hard, knowing he held something back. Harder still to act as though she hadn't felt it. For the first time all day, she didn't feel alone. And that surprised her more than she expected.

She returned home with the sea wind still in her hair and Quinton's warning echoing in her mind. He hadn't said much, but she'd seen enough to know he was holding something back. And not just for his own sake. That unsettled her more than she cared to admit.

Rodney arrived later that afternoon, unannounced but confident, as always. Mary-Ann had just slipped on her gloves and reached for her shawl when the butler announced him.

"I thought we might walk," Rodney said brightly. "The weather's quite fine."

"I have tea with Mrs. Bainbridge," she said, motioning toward the clock. "I'm expected shortly."

"No need to worry," he said with a wave of his hand. "I've taken care of that."

She blinked. "Taken care?" The words felt foreign in her mouth, as if something had been decided for her while she wasn't looking.

"I thought it prudent," he said smoothly, "to arrange for a companion. A lady's maid. She'll accompany you for errands and such. It's not quite fitting for you to be wandering about alone. And she's already met with Mrs. Bainbridge and rescheduled your tea for tomorrow."

Mary-Ann blinked, stunned not just by the assumption but by the timing. She had intended to review the latest bills of lading that morning. Cross-reference them against the weights from the *Redwake's* manifest. Now, with a stranger installed in her shadow and her schedule upended, that plan dissolved like steam from the kettle.

Mary-Ann stood very still. Rodney didn't seem to notice her stillness, or he chose not to. He forged ahead as if her silence were agreement.

"You arranged my schedule. Without asking."

"It's for your own ease, darling. Things will be different once we're married. You won't have to concern yourself with all these…details."

It wasn't kindness. It was dismissal, wrapped in lace.

She managed a smile, cool and distant. "How thoughtful."

He didn't notice the ice beneath it.

Mary-Ann didn't remind him that she wasn't his wife yet. But the thought struck, sharp and cold. Nor did she argue. Not yet. But something in her had shifted. It was subtle, like the first breath before a storm. Rodney thought he was protecting her. In truth, he was fencing her in, and she'd never taken kindly to cages.

Rodney, pleased with himself, left shortly after.

Mary-Ann did not watch him go. Instead, she sat alone in the quiet that followed, letting the day settle like dust around her. There was much she could not say. But more, so much more, that she would no longer allow to be taken from her. Not her judgment. Not her freedom. And certainly not the shape of her own life.

Mrs. Bainbridge arrived the next morning at Seaton House with a bouquet of crumpled correspondence and an air of high distress.

"We can't possibly set a date until Lord Maythorne confirms his travel plans. And now Lady Pomeroy is threatening to host a musical on the second of next month!" She dropped one letter onto the sitting room table, then another, as if the very paper betrayed her. "If we wait too long, we'll be buried under satin and scandal."

Mary-Ann, watching from the doorway, smiled faintly. "Surely not a scandal."

"Certainly a scandal," Mrs. Bainbridge huffed. Then, as if remembering, she pulled a narrow envelope from her reticule. "Oh, this arrived at the school. A donation for the Lifeboat Trust Fund, I believe. I didn't find any note inside."

She handed the envelope to Mary-Ann without a second thought.

Mary-Ann's fingers closed around the envelope. A curious

mark pressed into the wax caught her eye, a bird with its wings spread on a diamond-shaped design.

Her smile faded. She'd seen it before. Not in any manifest, but in the margins of the cloth-bound booklet Hamish had hidden. This was the same symbol.

She ran her thumb across the seal, pulse ticking louder in her throat.

She drew a slow breath, heart steady now with purpose. If one had found its way to her, others would too. And this time, she would be watching.

Chapter Twenty-One

THAT SAME TUESDAY, just after tea, the hush of the afternoon carried a promise of change.

"Good afternoon, Miss Seaton. Did you enjoy your tea with Mrs. Bainbridge?" asked the maid with a practiced curtsy.

"Yes, thank you. Very much so."

"Shall I set out your day dress or something more suitable for a walk?" the maid waited for her reply.

Mary-Ann paused in the doorway, studying the young woman. She was neat and trim, with a sharp nose and an even sharper air of certainty, not at all what she expected from a proper lady's maid.

"I don't believe we've been introduced."

"Apologies, miss. I'm Lydia Finch. Mr. Wilkinson arranged it all. I'm here to accompany you throughout the day, to appointments, errands, and whatever else you may need."

Mary-Ann stepped fully into the hall and let the door click softly behind her. "And what exactly do you consider your duties, Miss Finch?"

The girl blinked, then smiled with a hint of condescension. "Why, to ensure you don't tire yourself with the finer points of a busy household. To offer companionship, of course. And to keep you properly attended when you go about. It wouldn't do to have you wandering alone, now would it?"

There was something off in the smile, too knowing, too sure.

"I see," Mary-Ann said, her tone carefully neutral. "And I

assume you're familiar with my schedule?"

"As much as is proper, miss. Mr. Wilkinson was very clear."

"I'm sure he was."

Lydia tilted her head, clearly expecting agreement or gratitude.

Mary-Ann offered neither. Instead, she smiled softly. "Well, Miss Finch, I thank you for your eagerness. However, I will require some time this morning to review the correspondence. It's a quiet task, and I've no need for assistance."

"Very good, miss. I'll be just in the next room, should you need anything."

Mary-Ann offered a nod but did not retreat into the study at once. Instead, she turned down the corridor toward her father's study, not the sitting room Lydia had likely expected. If the maid noted the change in direction, she said nothing. Mary-Ann stepped into her father's study and waited until the door clicked shut behind her.

The study still carried a faint scent of pipe smoke and lavender wax polish, underscored by the quiet imprint of her father's order and quiet diligence, everything knew its place. Mary-Ann stood by the hearth, the same place she had stood so many evenings when she was younger, watching him leaf through ledgers with ink-stained fingers and a furrowed brow. But now the fire was unlit, and the room seemed to echo with everything that had changed.

She crossed to the desk, absently touching the blotter, then glanced toward the door. She paused. Her gaze shifted to the far wall instead. She stared at it for several seconds, the corners of her mouth lifting just slightly. Of course.

There had always been another way.

She moved to the panel near the hearth, where the paint had warped ever so slightly over the years. With a soft press, the jib door gave way. She didn't linger. Whatever comfort the room once held had turned hollow. As she stepped through the narrow passage, she paused just shy of the anteroom that opened behind the study.

From within, she paused at the antechamber jib door, catching the faint sound of light snoring. Lydia, it seemed, was less alert than she liked to appear.

A slow smile curved her lips. So, the woman made a habit of napping on duty. That was… useful.

She moved silently past, not disturbing a single floorboard, and followed the narrow path she had known well since childhood all the way upstairs and into her bed chamber.

She crossed her bedroom, her heart steady, her movements careful. The old ledger was still tucked on her shelf, disguised behind a row of dull, untouched volumes. She lifted it with care and turned to the wall beside the fireplace, the one with the faint seam in the wainscoting, just behind the dressing screen, a space she had discovered as a child, and which had kept its secret all these years.

With a firm press near the edge, the small compartment gave way.

For a moment, she feared it would be gone, that someone had discovered the hollow, and that when she opened the panel, she would find only dust. But the booklet was still there, plain and unassuming, yet pulsing with secrets. Relief and dread tangled in her chest.

She eased it out and settled at the desk, pulling the heavy drapes just enough to filter the morning light. She opened her private list of weight discrepancies, compiled weeks ago in neat, exacting columns, and began to cross-reference it with the entries marked by strange symbols in the back of the ledger.

Not all the symbols matched. Some were dots, slashes, or triangles, meaningless on their own. But then she saw it again.

The raven.

Drawn in hurried lines, wings outstretched over a diamond shape. Her breath caught for just a moment. The mark wasn't random. It wasn't decorative. It appeared beside three entries, each one tied to a shipment she had already flagged in her private notes. Two had passed through ships not listed in the official manifests.

This wasn't theory anymore. It was proof.

Her fingers rested lightly on the page, as though any sudden motion might break the thread she'd just uncovered.

She flipped to another page. There it was again. This time, next to a name she didn't recognize. Below it, another line: Percival Trent, in small, impersonal script.

She frowned, not because the name meant anything, but because so few of the entries had names at all. This one seemed oddly… tidy. She made no note of it and turned the page.

Beneath the entry, faintly, she saw another set of initials.

The handwriting had changed. It wasn't her father's, nor the loopy script Hamish had used. But it was familiar.

Wren.

She remembered the carved whalebone in her father's desk. Wren had given it to Hamish years ago, and she now kept it tucked away on the mantel. A quiet token. She had never given it much thought until now.

Her hand hesitated over the page. Was Wren warning them? Or had someone else taken up the book after him? The possibility opened like a cold draft through the room.

She flipped back to the last page and ran her finger along the bottom edge. There, pressed into the crease, was another raven. Smaller this time. Almost hidden.

Mary-Ann closed the book slowly, her fingers resting on the cover for a long breath. A part of her wanted to march to Barrington's estate this instant to demand answers from the only man who might understand the implications. Another part, quieter, steelier, held her still.

Quinton had looked at her yesterday with something close to fear, not fear of her, but fear for her. And that, more than anything, told her there were pieces of this puzzle even he was holding back.

She no longer believed this was simply a matter of mislogged cargo or clerical oversight. This was intentional. It was coordinated. And someone had tried to hide it, even from her father.

She stood, returning the book to the compartment and closing it firmly. For a moment, she considered replacing it with something else, a blank booklet, perhaps, or one of her old journals. A decoy. But the thought felt too theatrical. No one was rifling through her belongings. Not yet. And if they were... A knock on her bedchamber door startled her.

"Miss?" the maid's voice called, muffled.

Mary-Ann swallowed. "One moment."

She dusted her hands and pulled open the door.

"You weren't in the study," Lydia said, her tone carrying a mild reprimand, her brow pinching faintly.

Mary-Ann offered a soft smile. "I went to the antechamber but didn't want to disturb your rest."

A faint flush rose on Lydia's cheeks but was quickly smoothed over with a brittle smile. "Shall I help you prepare for your walk?"

"No," Mary-Ann said softly. "That won't be necessary today."

She stepped past the maid, her mind still with the raven, the diamond, and the name she didn't recognize. Lydia's smile tightened, but she stepped back with practiced grace. Mary-Ann didn't miss the flicker of calculation behind her eyes or the swift recalibration of a woman who had expected obedience and found something else entirely. She said nothing, but Mary-Ann made note of it, the second time the maid had tried to keep her contained. Once might be a habit. Twice was a strategy. Mary-Ann felt the presence at her back like a hush in a chapel. She had too many questions now to be chaperoned. Too many shadows were circling, and none of them would pause for a lady's maid.

And she was done waiting for permission to find the answers.

THE STUDY AT Sommer Chase was dimly lit, with thick drapes

drawn to guard against the late-morning sun. Barrington stood near the sideboard, two glasses untouched at his elbow. He didn't look up when the door opened.

"You said it was urgent," Quinton said, stepping inside.

"It is." Barrington turned, brows furrowed. "She was at the *Redwake* yesterday."

Quinton's jaw tensed. "You saw her?"

"I didn't have to. One of mine warned her off."

The air between them thickened.

"You had a man placed on the crew," Quinton said slowly. "And you didn't think to mention it?"

Barrington's expression didn't shift. "He was placed to watch for symbols. Movements. And yes, people. She was never meant to get that close."

Quinton crossed to the window and looked out, jaw set. "And yet she did."

"Because she's clever. And determined. You knew she would push."

"Yes," Quinton said, turning. "And you knew I would want to protect her."

Barrington moved to the desk and rested his hands on the edge. "You're not thinking clearly. She's not some ally in your old campaigns. This is something darker. Deeper."

"She's not an ally," Quinton said. "She's the reason I survived those campaigns."

The silence that followed was sharp.

Barrington exhaled. "The Order has threads in places we haven't even mapped yet. I won't risk dragging her into that."

"You already have," Quinton said.

That gave Barrington pause.

"She saw the symbol." Quinton stepped closer. "And we both know what that means. She's involved whether you like it or not."

Barrington's voice dropped. "She doesn't know what it means."

"Not yet."

Barrington studied him. "Then let's keep it that way."

Quinton didn't respond. Not immediately. His jaw tensed as he gazed fixed on the window, though the light blurred more than it revealed. He turned back to the window, gazing out at the sea beyond the rise.

"Do I have your word, Captain?"

Quinton's posture straightened. "You do."

But his reflection in the glass told a different story: the tightness in his shoulders, the set of his jaw, and the slow clench of his hands.

He'd meant every word until now.

He had given Barrington a promise. But it was Mary-Ann's trust he feared losing. That was the oath he couldn't bear to break, because deep down, he knew he had already.

He would protect her. But there would come a moment, a tipping point. He would know when it arrived. And if the truth could no longer be contained, he would be the one to give it to her. Not because Barrington ordered it. But because he owed her that much. Even if it meant protecting her from the lies they told in her name.

Chapter Twenty-Two

WEDNESDAY MORNING, WITH the sea unusually still and every silence laden with unspoken truths, the day began. The mist had not yet burned off the river, and Sommer-by-the-Sea lay quiet beneath its veil, unaware, perhaps, that decisions made far from its cobbled streets were shaping its fate.

The room was quiet, save for the hiss of wax dripping onto stone. No names were spoken. None were needed.

A single candle burned in the center of the long table, its flame reflected in the eyes of four shadowed figures. The scent of damp earth and cold iron clung to the chamber. They had met here before beneath the city, beneath suspicion. Always in darkness.

One leaned forward, gloved fingers steepled. "Glasgow is secure. The warehouse is operational again, and the inquiry has been reassigned to one of our members."

"And France?"

"The customs delay was arranged through the harbormaster's clerk in Calais. We were able to gain two weeks, and everything we needed was moved."

"Spain required more finesse," another said, his voice low. "A fire took the rest. There'll be no audit. The building was declared unsalvageable."

There was a pause as if a collective breath was drawn.

"London is proving less cooperative. Parliament is divided. But progress has been made. Two more have pledged support."

"And the trading houses?"

A third speaker, older, with a raspy tone, gave a thin smile. "Four are compromised. One is owned outright. Seaton's influence is waning, and his debts are growing. Wilkinson is being groomed and shows promise."

"And yet," said the one seated at the head, "Barrington's Brigade continues to interfere."

A hush followed the name.

"They've embedded well," another said. "But the operation involving the *Redwake* was not exposed. Our man reported no disruptions. Only a local woman sniffing about."

"She was identified?"

"No. He said she claimed to be fetching a package for her mistress. It was dismissed."

"And his loyalty?"

"Proven. He knows the lines not to cross."

"Should we confirm her name?"

"Not yet," the leader said. If she's what she claims to be, there's no need to pique her interest. If not, she'll come closer."

"Curiosity," murmured the first speaker, "is like rot. Left unchecked, it spreads."

"And our long-term goals?"

The leader's voice was low but commanding. "Order. Stability. But only through the hands we choose. These governments were not built for permanence. They were built for profit. We will give them both at a cost they do not yet recognize."

"And when they do?"

"It will be too late."

The others murmured in agreement.

"Sommer-by-the-Sea is small, but it has roots in shipping and the routes we need. The influence we can mold. The Seaton girl is a distraction, not a threat. And Seaton has nearly outlived his usefulness."

"Wilkinson will be in place by the end of the season."

A silence followed, thin, watchful, and calculated.

"I still question the wisdom of it," came a new voice, sharp and clipped. "Wilkinson is too self-assured. He makes errors and covers them with arrogance."

"He's useful," another replied. "He thinks he's climbing the ranks. Let him. So long as he never learns who's holding the ladder."

The leader shifted slightly. "We've kept tighter men for less. If he fails to deliver the town's ports, we'll remove him."

"And Barrington?" someone else asked. "He's cost us two courier lines and a contact in the Ministry. His Brigade is becoming more than inconvenient."

"Barrington won't stop," the elder rasped. "He's a relic of another age, honor, duty, all that rot."

"Should we pull out of Sommer-by-the-Sea?"

"No," the leader said. "It's already in motion. The girl, the debts, the docks. We're closer here than most realize. Let them underestimate us."

The candle hissed louder. Then, the light was snuffed, and the room returned to silence.

Across town, in a house full of windows and morning light, Mary-Ann sat with a teacup cooling in her hand, unaware of the meeting held in shadows or the ways in which her name had nearly been spoken.

Her chair had been angled just enough to catch the morning light, but it did little to lift the unease curling low in her stomach. The scent of toast and orange marmalade lingered in the air, untouched. A maid moved quietly in the background, straightening the silver at the sideboard. Across the table, a place had been set for her father, though he hadn't yet appeared.

The tick of the longcase clock in the hallway marked each moment with practiced civility, but the silence between ticks stretched oddly this morning. She used to relish mornings like this, quiet and predictable, but now the quiet felt deceptive.

Lydia sat opposite her, sipping tea with calculated leisure. "Will your father be joining us?"

"Not this morning." Mary-Ann didn't elaborate.

"A shame. I was hoping he might be convinced to walk with us today. The weather is fine, and a little sea air does wonders for the nerves."

Mary-Ann smiled, not kindly. "You may walk without me if you need some air."

Lydia blinked, caught off guard. "Oh. I'd only meant, well, it might be more cheerful if we—"

"Thank you, but no," Mary-Ann said.

Across the room, the latest issue of the *Sommer Sentinel* lay folded open, its headline just visible from where she sat.

"The Dragon's Wake," read the headline. "Young Buccaneers Tell Their Story of Being Rescued from Sommer's Hidden Caves."

She rose and crossed to it.

The article took a lighthearted tone, built around the boys' own version of events. They claimed to be young buccaneers on a treasure hunt, armed with a wooden sword and a sack of raisins. But their story, however innocent, unfolded alongside details that left Mary-Ann uneasy. They had wandered deep into the caves during low tide and were rescued just as the water began to rise.

One of the rescuers was quoted as saying the cave had been unusually cleared out as though someone had been through just ahead of them.

It was the final paragraph that caught her attention.

"Rescuers reported broken boards and debris strewn inside the cave, likely remnants of fishing or smuggling operations long abandoned. One plank bore the faded letters 'DWA.' Evidence, perhaps, that a dragon's hoard now scattered by the sea."

Mary-Ann's brow furrowed. DWA. She read it again. Slowly. Redwake.

She pressed a hand to the table's edge. The boys had gone looking for dragons, but what had they nearly found instead? The article called it whimsy. She saw something else. If a child could stumble into danger that easily, what else had passed unnoticed?

Had she been wrong to let it go, to think she had more time?

She wondered how long the cave had been used and how many others had wandered too close. She folded the Sentinel and put it on the sideboard.

Mr. Hollis quietly entered the room, carrying a folded note on a tray. "A message from Mrs. Bainbridge."

From behind her, Lydia's voice rang out. "Planning a seaside outing, miss?"

"*Miss* Finch," Mr. Hollis corrected gently, "the young lady is addressed as *Miss Seaton*."

Lydia flushed, then dipped into a curtsy that was a beat too late.

"Thank you, Mr. Hollis." Mary-Ann took the note from the tray and read it.

She looked up at the maid. "I was just reading, Miss Finch." Mary-Ann carefully folded the note and tucked it into her pocket.

"I imagine it must be dull, all this quiet," Lydia said sweetly. "I could arrange a call for you. I understand that Lady Alverton is in town."

"Lady Alverton is seventy-nine and has not left her drawing room in a decade."

Lydia blinked. "Oh. I must have been mistaken. One of the housemaids mentioned her," Lydia added quickly. "She said Lady Alverton was a friend of the family."

Mary-Ann's gaze didn't waver. "She was. Once."

The silence that followed wasn't sharp, but it was deliberate.

Mary-Ann's smile was cool. "Do you like to read, Miss Finch? Or do you prefer embroidery?"

"Oh, I don't do much of either," Lydia replied lightly. "I find the days more enjoyable when they're spent in cheerful company."

"And what about cards?"

Lydia's smile tightened. "Only if the company is of a genteel sort."

Mary-Ann tilted her head. "I'll keep that in mind."

She excused herself. As she passed one of the footmen, she caught a faint roll of his eyes as Lydia walked behind her.

Interesting. Not everyone, it seemed, was pleased with Miss Finch's presence. And that, too, was useful.

But it left Mary-Ann uneasy. Lydia had threaded herself through the household quickly. She knew the rhythms of the staff and inserted herself into their errands, their tea breaks, and their comings and goings. And yet, the signs of strain were beginning to show. She noticed the pinched expressions, the glances that lingered too long. The smallest cracks in a surface too carefully smoothed. She would have to keep watch. Quietly.

She didn't go far. At the base of the stairs, Mary-Ann paused beside the tall front window. Sunlight spilled across the polished floor, gilding the quiet edges of the morning. She touched the windowsill, absently tracing the grain of the wood.

The boys had gone searching for dragons, but someone had been there first. Someone connected to the Redwake. And Quinton...

He had warned her to be careful. Not out of habit, not protectively, but because he knew something he hadn't yet said. She pressed her hand to the cool glass. *Not yet,* he'd told her.

He hadn't told her everything. That much was clear. But he hadn't lied either. Not with his eyes. Not with his silence.

He'd tried to protect her. She didn't doubt that. But what he hadn't said might matter more than what he had.

And the trouble was... she believed him.

But belief was not the same as surrender. She didn't need reassurance. She needed proof.

She could feel the shape of something forming, subtle as a bruise beneath the surface. It was in the letters, the ships, the stories no one finished. A shadow pulling at every thread.

She would find the next piece. Quietly. Just long enough to get close.

Chapter Twenty-Three

TUESDAY MORNING, SUNLIGHT streamed through the parlor windows as Mrs. Bainbridge declared war on the guest list "I simply cannot send invitations to a wedding that doesn't exist yet." Mrs. Bainbridge dropped a folio of pressed writing paper onto the table like a general slamming down a campaign map. Cream and ivory sheets, each bearing a different hand-pressed border or embossed crest. None of it would matter until a date and venue were decided.

"I have a cousin who was married in the rain," she added. She had planned for sunshine and roses, but ended up with mud and mildew. *Do you know what saved it?*"

Mary-Ann smiled faintly. "Love?"

"Cloaks and parasols," Mrs. Bainbridge declared. "The footmen dashed out with anything they could find, shawls, rugs, parasols from the drawing room. The guests were half-drowned and laughing like sailors. But the poor girl never forgave the weather, or her mother."

Mary-Ann stifled a laugh. "You sound prepared for anything."

"I was," she said. "Until I met him. Barrington rearranged every plan I'd ever made just by standing still long enough to be admired."

There was a pause, not quite tender but close enough. Then Mrs. Bainbridge sniffed and resumed flipping through the paper as if nothing at all had been confessed.

Mary-Ann, seated near the window, offered a sympathetic

smile. "I'm sure the delay is only temporary."

"*Temporary,*" Mrs. Bainbridge echoed. She tossed the word into the air like a handkerchief with a tear in it. "You say that as if it means anything. As if Barrington isn't dodging my questions with the same skill he once used to avoid his mother's pianoforte recitals."

Mary-Ann tried for a soothing tone. "I'm sure he's not dodging."

"He's strategizing," Lydia added sweetly, gliding in with a small tray of tea as if summoned by gossip. "It's a sign of a thoughtful man."

Mrs. Bainbridge blinked, her brows lifting. "*Is it?*"

Mary-Ann bit the inside of her cheek to keep from smiling.

"I have two homes in London," Mrs. Bainbridge declared, gesturing broadly, though she ignored the tea tray entirely. "His lordship has one. Perfectly suitable, and yet he says he's considering something else."

"What else?" Mary-Ann asked, leaning forward slightly.

Mrs. Bainbridge sighed, the kind of sigh that summoned storms. "Rosalynde Bay."

That caught Mary-Ann off guard. She blinked. "Truly?"

"Where we met, he says. *Where it all began.*"

"That's... rather romantic." Lydia offered.

"It is also," Mrs. Bainbridge said, slicing the air with one hand, "miles from anywhere, and entirely unsuitable for a guest list that includes no fewer than two duchesses and one very inconvenient baroness who is allergic to sea air."

Mary-Ann tried not to laugh, but a quiet breath of amusement escaped. "And yet you love him."

Mrs. Bainbridge dropped her chin to her chest in mock defeat. "Worse. I agreed to marry him."

Lydia gave a light chuckle. "You'll find a compromise. Love always does."

Mrs. Bainbridge gave her a long look. "I sincerely hope you're right, Miss Finch. Though I've found love is much like planning a wedding. It looks lovely on paper, but then it stamps its boots through your best-laid table arrangements.

Mary-Ann offered to help pack away the samples. Lydia lingered for another few minutes, making soft observations and asking a few too many questions about the guest list, before excusing herself to retrieve a shawl.

As her footsteps faded down the hall, Mrs. Bainbridge exhaled and turned toward the window. "I have the oddest urge to scatter her," she murmured.

Mary-Ann blinked and paused mid-fold. "Scatter her?"

"Like dandelion fluff."

That earned a laugh. "You're in fine form today."

"No one in this house quite remembers how to be themselves when you're around, my dear," Mrs. Bainbridge said, adjusting a stack of samples with casual precision. Her voice softened. "You bring out the truth in people. I find it refreshing."

Mary-Ann didn't speak at first. She simply smiled, her fingers resting lightly on the edge of the table. There were many things she wasn't certain of these days, but this, she would carry with her.

MRS. BAINBRIDGE LEFT, and Mary-Ann followed shortly after, claiming a headache. It was polite enough to be unassailable, vague enough to buy her time. As she passed through the hallway, she caught sight of Lydia in the mirror above the sideboard, still tidying her sleeve as if rehearsing the next moment of charm. It gave Mary-Ann just enough time. She wasn't sure if it was the conversation or the sense that Lydia was always just a step behind her, smiling too sweetly, watching too closely. It left her breathless in a way no headache ever had.

She slipped on her gloves and took the back path out of the house, lifting her skirts slightly to keep them from the morning dew. The spring breeze was mild, the sky a soft, steady blue. A line of gulls danced along the roof of a fishmonger's shop, their wings flashing white and silver.

Her heart had steadied by the time she turned past the churchyard, but her mind had not. Each step echoed evenings long past. Those shared walks, shoulder to shoulder, when Quinton would match his pace to hers without a word. She didn't go to the harbor. Not yet. She took the path to the rise as they once had, not because she expected him there but because sometimes hope took the shape of old habits. Instead, she took the narrow path up the rise beyond the churchyard, where the view of the sea made the world feel both wide and still.

He stood there as he had all those years ago.

Quinton stood near the stone wall, coat unbuttoned, hands tucked behind his back. He didn't turn when she approached, though she saw his shoulders shift.

"I hope I'm not intruding," she said softly.

He turned, and the moment their eyes met, something in her chest realigned.

"No," he said. "Only waiting."

"For what?"

He didn't look surprised to see her. As if he'd expected this moment long before it arrived. "I'm not entirely sure."

She joined him at the wall, silence stretching comfortably between them. The sea churned far below, each wave rising and folding like breath.

"Barrington said the *Redwake* left port yesterday morning," she said at last.

"I know."

She hesitated. "There was a shipment manifest I never saw. I'm certain it existed and that I was meant to review the weights."

"I heard," he said quietly.

She studied him. "You're gathering information."

"So are you."

The corner of his mouth twitched slightly, as if he wanted to say more, to confess that seeing her like this, here, searching and brave, made it harder not to tell her everything.

A flicker of acknowledgment passed between them, the smallest thread of understanding. And yet something still hovered unspoken between them.

He looked away first, his gaze drifting toward the horizon. "Some things aren't ready to be named."

"But they're there," she said. "Aren't they?"

He met her eyes again, and the pause between them held more than words could carry.

"Quinton." Her voice was low. "Why won't you tell me what you know?"

He didn't answer immediately. The breeze tugged at the hem of her coat. "I don't want to bring you into something dangerous," he said finally.

"You think I'm not already in it?"

His jaw tightened.

"I'm not made of glass, you know," she added, softer now.

"No," he said. "You're made of fire. You shine so brightly, sometimes I think you don't realize it burns."

She blinked.

He turned to face her fully. His gaze was steady. "That's why I worry. Because you'll walk straight into the flame to see what's burning."

She hadn't meant for it to happen. But since the moment he stepped into her entrance hall, tired, changed, and alive, something inside her had been drifting toward the flame. She hadn't stopped it, and she didn't want to.

She tried to smile, but it faltered. "I thought I lost you."

"You didn't."

Her hand lifted, hovering for a breath before she touched his sleeve. She didn't say more, not about the past or what they'd lost. The ache in her chest was answer enough.

The silence was different now, dense and full of words they weren't brave enough to say yet.

She leaned in first. Or perhaps he did. Later, she wouldn't be sure.

Their second kiss was not hesitant. It wasn't rushed. It bloomed like something inevitable, forged from nights of silence and days of aching possibility. His hand found her waist, drawing her just close enough to feel the echo of her breath. Her fingers curled into the lapel of his coat, not to steady herself, but to hold onto something she hadn't realized she'd missed.

The kiss was firm and unguarded, a quiet collision of longing and recognition. It deepened as he tilted his head, and her lips parted without fear. It was not a question. It was a vow.

There had been a time when she thought this part of herself was gone, the part that felt deeply, without fear. But he had brought it back with nothing more than a look, a silence, a kiss that said everything neither of them dared name. It wasn't new. It was old, aching, and inevitable.

He remembered the first kiss, windy and stolen in the hush of morning, her lips trembling with more surprise than certainty. This one was different. She met him fully now. No tremble. Just heat.

And for one long moment, they forgot the world entirely.

She stepped back slowly, her breath uneven.

"We can't keep doing that," she said.

"Then tell me to stop."

She didn't. Not yet. Not when it still felt like the truth.

Chapter Twenty-Four

WEDNESDAY MORNING, SUSPICION sat heavier than the fog beyond the windows. Mary-Ann had no proof. No confession. No names. Only the weight of instinct, sharpened by ledger entries and half-truths. And now, one more whisper: the cave.

The choice to go alone wasn't made lightly. But if she'd learned anything over the past weeks, it was that no one else would show her the truth. Rodney thought she was best suited for drawing rooms and decorum. Barrington believed secrets were best held behind closed doors. And Quinton—

She stopped that thought before it could settle. His silence stung, but it was his loyalty to Barrington that had tied his hands, not a lack of caring.

Still, she needed answers. And this time, she wouldn't ask permission.

She stood before the mirror in her room, fingers gripping the sides of the washstand as if bracing against the tide of her own uncertainty. Her reflection stared back. She was drawn and pale, but steady.

"You must go," she whispered. It felt foolish, speaking aloud, but there was no one else she could say it to. No one else who might offer courage. She straightened her shoulders and lifted her chin. "You've done harder things."

Still, her hands didn't feel brave. Her breath stuttered as she reached for the basket. Maybe courage wasn't boldness at all.

Maybe it was doing the next thing even while afraid.

And if not, if she hadn't been brave before, then perhaps this moment, this choice, this quiet action in the face of fear would be her first true act of courage.

With one last glance, she turned and crossed the room, her steps quiet and firm. It was time.

She opened the *Sommer Sentinel* again, fingers smoothing the page more out of habit than need. She'd read the article twice already, but this time, she read between the lines.

Two boys rescued from a coastal cave, the tide rising behind them. They'd wandered in with a stick and a tin spyglass, claiming dragons, treasure, and a cave that "breathed with the sea."

The reporter called it whimsy. But Mary-Ann had learned to listen differently.

Disturbed stones. Broken boards were swept to one side. A faint marking "dwa," almost lost to salt and time. She'd seen it before, in Hamish's ledger. But here, in stone, it confirmed what she'd only suspected.

Redwake.

The sea hadn't washed everything away. And what remained, remained for a reason.

⟫⟩⟩⟨⟨⟨

SHE LEFT THE house just past noon, claiming an errand and choosing her moment carefully. The air in the sitting room had grown drowsy. Lydia was half-asleep in the corner chair, a half-embroidered napkin drooping from her lap and her head lolling slightly to one side. She murmured something unintelligible as Mary-Ann passed but didn't stir. Good. The woman had a habit of dozing when not watched, and Mary-Ann had quietly begun cataloging the fact.

Her father had retreated to his study, the door shut tight.

Mrs. Bainbridge had gone to the seamstress, armed with stern opinions and a fraying patience.

Mary-Ann crossed the hall with quiet purpose, each step carefully placed. At the last moment, she turned back, retrieved the folded newspaper from her father's desk, and tucked it into the basket beneath her gloves. One last look. Just in case.

Mary-Ann wore her sturdiest boots and a walking coat she hadn't used in weeks. In a small basket, she carried a folded oilskin, a pair of gloves, and a lantern she'd prepared in advance. The wick trimmed, oil-filled, and a small flint striker tucked into the base. She'd tested it earlier that morning behind the greenhouse, striking the flint until the wick caught with a tiny bloom of light.

She took the long path past the edge of town, passing under a crooked arch of hawthorn branches, then followed a sheep trail that twisted downward from the cliffs toward the beach below. It was steep, uneven, and damp from the morning mist. Brambles clawed at her skirts, and the sole of her right boot slipped once on a patch of shale, sending her heart into her throat.

She paused there, steadying herself on a jutting stone. The wind had picked up, tugging at her bonnet and making the edges of the basket bump against her hip. Still, she kept going.

The sea stretched out ahead, silver-gray and restless. And there, half veiled by a bend in the stone, the cave.

Her hands trembled slightly as she descended the last dozen steps, which were more worn down by water than by human feet. The shore here was littered with smooth pebbles and the occasional tangled net.

The cave's opening loomed ahead, dark and wide against the pale sand, tucked beneath a jagged overhang. The wind had died here, and the silence settled like fog.

She hesitated. Fear pricked her, sharp and sudden. What if someone was already inside? What if she found something she couldn't explain? Or worse. What if she found nothing at all?

She hovered at the edge, where light met dark, unsure if she was about to step into clarity or vanish completely. The air changed here. It always did before something important happened.

She exhaled slowly and pulled the lantern from her basket. Her fingers shook as she struck the flint, once, then twice. The wick flared to life, casting an amber halo around her feet.

One step. Then another. She stepped inside. The cave swallowed her whole.

The air shifted instantly. It was cooler, damp, and tinged with the smell of salt and earth. Her footsteps echoed softly, brushing up against the stone walls like whispers. The lantern's glow reached only a few feet ahead, the rest consumed by shadow. Her pulse tapped against her throat.

Every childhood story about smugglers and secret passages returned in half-formed fragments, except this wasn't a tale. This was real. Her breath caught as the sound of the sea filtered through the stone. It wasn't a roar, but a rhythmic hush, as if the cave itself were breathing.

She hesitated, the silence pressing in around her, then she moved forward, deeper into the dark.

THE FIRST CAVERN was wide and dark, the walls slick with sea residue. Water pooled in uneven hollows. As she moved, her light threw shifting shadows across the stone, and the echo of her footsteps made the space feel larger than it was. She ventured farther in.

The back chamber was narrower, the ceiling lower. But it was clean. Too clean. No driftwood. No seaweed. No broken shells. The ground bore faint scrapes, drag marks, and a slight indentation, as though something heavy had rested there.

She crouched, running her fingers along the stone. Smoothed by water. Or by crates.

A perfect place to offload cargo. The tide would rise, erase it all just as it had with the children.

She turned to go, but her boot caught on to something. She stumbled forward, bracing herself on one hand. Her lantern swung wildly but didn't fall.

Cursing softly, she crouched to inspect the snag. A rock, she thought, but no, it was loose. She nudged it aside and found a coil of rope, partially buried in a recess between the stones. Heavy. Used.

Her heart hammered.

Evidence. Real, tangible evidence. It wasn't her imagination. She hadn't chased shadows into the dark. There was something here. Someone had used this cave. Recently. And not just once. A flicker of elation bloomed beneath her ribs, nearly dizzying. She was right.

But it faded quickly, replaced by the need to conceal it. She had no idea who might return, or when. She replaced the rock carefully, fingers trembling now for a different reason.

She rose and turned back toward the entrance, the lantern steady in her grip, her heart still fluttering with the thrill of discovery. She brushed the grit from her palms and started back toward the cave's entrance.

⫸⫷

THE DAYLIGHT BEYOND was blinding. Her eyes had adjusted to the gloom, and the sudden glare made the world flatten. She stepped forward straight into something solid. Hard. Unyielding. A wall. No, a man.

She gasped, stumbling back with a sharp cry. The lantern flared wildly, its light swinging in a trembling arc. Panic seized her chest. For one breathless second, she couldn't even form a name. There was only the pounding rush of fear in her ears.

"You don't belong here," a deep, low voice said.

Her breath caught in her throat. The light shifted.

"Quinton?" she managed.

His face came into view as the shadows fell away.

He didn't move. Didn't speak at first. His presence filled the space, as steady as the tide.

"You followed me."

"I was already here."

"How long?"

"Long enough to hate every second of it."

Mary-Ann steadied her breath, but the rapid pulse in her throat betrayed her. "Then you understand why I had to come."

His jaw shifted slightly. "You could have been seen."

"I wasn't."

"You don't know that," he said, his voice low, not angry, but tight with something unspoken. Fear, maybe. Or something closer to regret.

She did know. But she didn't argue with him.

He stepped aside so she could pass, but she didn't move immediately. The silence stretched, the sea murmuring behind them.

"You're angry," she said.

"I'm—" He exhaled. "I'm concerned for you."

Her voice softened. "I know."

Neither of them said a word.

"Next time," he said quietly, "I'll go with you."

She hadn't expected him to say it. Not so plainly. But maybe that was how they moved forward now. No more riddles, no more waiting. Just the truth, spoken quietly.

She met his gaze, a flicker of surprise in her eyes.

He didn't smile. He didn't need to. The promise was there, unspoken.

She nodded once and walked past him, into the light.

He watched her silhouette merge with the light, his pulse still thudding like he hadn't fully let her go.

He didn't follow. Not yet. He stood there a moment longer,

listening to the sea, trying to slow the fear that hadn't left him since she stepped inside. He hadn't known how deeply it would gut him to see her disappear into darkness. She was brilliant, stubborn, and recklessly brave. None of that made her invincible.

He pressed a hand against the cave wall, grounding himself and reminding himself that she was safe. For now.

Chapter Twenty-Five

WEDNESDAY AFTERNOON, THE wind tugged at her cloak as she stepped through Barrington's door unannounced. Mary-Ann had barely arrived at Barrington's townhouse when she was ushered into the drawing room and into the chaos that was Mrs. Bainbridge.

Barrington had been called away on urgent business, leaving the drawing room to suffer the full force of Mrs. Bainbridge's wedding preparations.

The room looked as though it had been swept up in a paper storm. Swatches of fabric, invitation samples, and half-filled teacups littered every available surface. A small pile of folded letters teetered on the edge of the pianoforte bench, and a lace-trimmed veil was draped unceremoniously over a bust of Cicero.

She had expected quiet. A moment to gather her thoughts. Instead, she was greeted by a tempest of lace, letters, and Latin indignation, Mrs. Bainbridge's dramatic fury over having to recite her vows in a language she neither spoke nor trusted.

Kenworth, predictably unruffled, stood by the fireplace inspecting a parchment scroll as if he were reviewing troop deployments.

She barely had time to cross the threshold before Mrs. Bainbridge descended upon her like a flurry of ribbon and distress.

"He suggested a bishop who only speaks Latin! Latin, Mary-Ann! I am not reciting vows in a language I don't even understand. What if I accidentally promise to become a hermit or a goose keeper?"

Mary-Ann blinked, stepping out of her walking boots as the woman pressed a sheaf of papers into her hands.

"And don't get me started on the menu. Her ladyship believes aspic is elegant. Aspic, Mary-Ann. Jellied vegetables pretending to be refined. If we serve it, I may simply perish before the vows are exchanged."

Sketches, guest lists, and what looked suspiciously like a diagram of the church's seating arrangement were among the papers in her hand. A tiny ink blot marked a prominent X labeled: *Duchess of Carrimere—DO NOT OFFEND.*

"I don't know why I bother planning anything when Barrington's mother undoes it all before I've finished my tea," Mrs. Bainbridge huffed, pulling off her gloves with dramatic flair. "And now she wants to move the ceremony to their London townhouse. I told her it would be easier to marry in the Tower of London. I think she thought I was serious."

Mary-Ann stifled a smile. The whirlwind of frustration and absurdity was almost comforting.

From the doorway, Kenworth cleared his throat. "If I may, madam, one rarely needs to raise one's voice in the Tower."

Mrs. Bainbridge narrowed her eyes. "You're enjoying this. And don't say only mildly. You have that particular look about you. It's the same one you had when I discovered you had swapped out Lord Pevensey's wine with claret vinegar at the summer ball."

"Only mildly."

"Mary-Ann, I'm going to need you to elope on my behalf. Take Quinton, take a carriage, and disappear to Gretna Green. Barrington and I will follow your example shortly."

Mary-Ann laughed, unable to help herself. "You could always suggest holding it at Rosalynde Bay," she teased. "It would certainly keep the duchesses guessing."

Mrs. Bainbridge paused. "Don't tempt me."

Kenworth arched a brow. "Scenic. Windblown. Remote. I

dare say the guest list would shrink accordingly."

Mary-Ann handed the seating chart back.

"You're not going to Gretna Green. You're going to marry Lord Barrington with every duchess in England watching, and they're going to weep into their lace gloves at how magnificent you look."

Mrs. Bainbridge's expression softened. "That is a very appealing image."

Then let's start by ensuring they all have chairs.

Kenworth murmured, "Preferably with name cards. Perhaps in English."

Mrs. Bainbridge let out a sigh and flopped into the nearest chair. "I shall write to that bishop myself and inform him that the ceremony will be conducted in one language only, and that language will not be Latin."

Mary-Ann grinned and turned toward the stairs, her heart lighter than it had been in weeks. Mrs. Bainbridge had stepped out a few moments earlier to speak with a potential new student, leaving the room and a rare patch of quiet behind.

※》》》※《《《※

SHE WAS STILL smiling when a quiet knock came at the corridor door.

The light from the afternoon sun slanted through the tall windows, gilding the edge of the carpet and the shimmer of the discarded invitation papers. Her fingers stilled as she turned, smoothing her skirt as though the knock had reached deeper than sound. It had a familiarity that warmed and unsettled all at once.

Not firm or urgent, just enough to be polite, and unmistakably familiar. Quinton stood there, looking as if he might have debated whether to knock a second time.

"I wasn't sure if this was a poor time," he said. "You were clearly under siege earlier."

"Only from bishops and lace," she replied, stepping back to let him in. "I've survived worse."

Quinton stepped inside, his gaze brushing over the folded sketches and guest lists still scattered across the table near the hearth. "I take it the Duchess of Carrimere remains unseated?"

"She's been moved seven times in two days. Kenworth believes her a greater tactical challenge than Napoleon."

That earned a quiet laugh. "He's not wrong."

There was a pause, not an awkward one, but a thoughtful one. The kind that came after something had changed. She laced her fingers together, uncertain.

"I didn't expect you," she said.

"No," Quinton replied. "But I thought perhaps you'd like this back." He held up a folded page, the *Sommer Sentinel*. "You left it behind."

She accepted it, the memory of the cave and the tide-laced wind flickering behind her eyes.

"Thank you," she murmured.

Quinton hesitated. "I know I have no right to ask, but… are you all right?"

Mary-Ann nodded. "I've learned to tread carefully. Not just in caves."

That pulled a smile from him. It was gentle but touched with something more. The kind of smile that belonged to late summer walks and quiet conversations in fading light, to moments so familiar they had become part of who she was.

"I used to walk with you nearly every evening," he said suddenly. "I don't think I appreciated what it meant at the time. Matching your pace. Letting you speak first. Listening."

Her throat tightened. "I remember."

She used to count the stars as they walked. His hand always hovered near but never quite touched hers. That restraint had meant something then. It still did.

He took a half-step closer. His voice dropped softer than she'd ever heard it. "I don't want to lose that again."

Her breath caught. She hadn't expected those words not

spoken aloud. Not yet. The moment hung between them. Not a kiss, but as good as one, threaded with memory and promise.

Mary-Ann's voice was soft, but steady. "Then walk with me again. Not in memory, Quinton. In truth. When it's time."

His jaw shifted slightly, as if that one invitation steadied him more than he'd admit.

He nodded once. "I'll be there."

⟫⟩⟨⟪

LATER THAT AFTERNOON, as Mary-Ann gathered her things to leave, a messenger from her father's office arrived with a letter.

"It was delivered to Seaton Shipping, miss. Mr. Jessop thought it might be important," he said. "Your butler, Mr. Hollis, said you were expected here."

She accepted the envelope, her name in a flowing script. "Thank you, Lewis." Her fingers stilled when she saw the seal, a deep, glossy black, stamped with the faint impression of a raven. No address, no signature.

She hesitated. The seal was too perfect, the color too dark. She'd seen wax like that once before. It was on a ledger she hadn't been meant to read.

She broke the wax and unfolded the note. It contained only one line:

"Some things wash in with the tide. Others are best left to drift away."

Her chest tightened.

To anyone else, it might seem like nothing. A scrap of philosophical nonsense. But to her, it was a warning.

She had seen that raven before. In the margins of the cloth-bound booklet, inked beside names and symbols that didn't belong in any respectable ledger. She felt a flicker of cold recognition, and with it, the slow coil of fear tightening low in her belly.

They know I saw it.

Her fingers trembled slightly as she refolded the message. She couldn't let anyone see her reaction. Not yet.

She folded the note and slipped it into her reticule. The words lived there now tucked against her side, whispering between each breath.

With practiced calm, she drew out a coin and glanced up at the footman, offering a faint smile. "Thank you." She handed the coin over without hesitation.

The air outside felt colder as if the message had followed her into the light. She was no longer smiling.

Chapter Twenty-Six

THURSDAY MORNING, THE sun had barely crested the rooftops when Lydia knocked on Mary-Ann's door with a list in hand and wearing a too-bright smile.

"Good morning, Miss Seaton. Mr. Wilkinson has asked that I accompany you today. He thought a walk through Bond Street might lift your spirits, followed by a visit to Madame Duclaire's for glove fittings and then tea at Lady Wrexley's. He's taken the liberty of arranging the entire afternoon."

Mary-Ann folded her hands calmly on the vanity table. "Has he?"

"Yes, miss." Lydia gave a practiced smile. "He was most insistent that today be restful. No appointments at the office."

A chill ran beneath Mary-Ann's skin. Her pulse flickered, calm, composed. This was how they meant to manage her, with gloves and teas and careful distractions. She looked at her reflection, at the composed woman she was meant to be. She remembered days when she had walked the docks without permission, tall and certain. Now even her footsteps were charted. "How thoughtful," she said lightly, rising to retrieve her shawl. "Still, I believe I'll stop at Seaton Shipping first."

She remembered Hamish's steady presence at the docks, and the way he taught her to read the tide as easily as a page. It was Hamish who told her that ink never lied, but the people behind it sometimes did. Those ledgers were her map now. And she would not be turned away from them.

Lydia hesitated. "But—"

"I'm sure Madame Duclaire won't mind a slight delay."

As they reached the foot of the stairs, the sharp knock at the front door halted them both. Mr. Hollis appeared from the corridor and opened it. A young runner in Seaton Shipping's livery stood panting on the step.

"For Miss Seaton," he said breathlessly, holding out a folded note. "Urgent. From the docks."

Mary-Ann read the message quickly. Her spine straightened. "I must go to the office. At once."

"Miss—" Lydia began.

Mary-Ann's voice was polite, but immovable. "Kindly let Mr. Wilkinson know I've chosen to go alone. I trust he will understand."

The carriage ride was quiet, save for the rhythmic clatter of hooves and the rustle of paper as Mary-Ann unfolded the note once more. Lydia had remained behind, her protests cut short by Mary-Ann's unflinching composure and Mr. Hollis's firm suggestion that the young woman might be more useful tending to tasks at home. Alone at last, Mary-Ann stared out the window, jaw tight, gloves folded in her lap.

He would have understood. Not Rodney, not Lydia, but Quinton. She could almost hear his voice, that maddening calm, asking what she meant to do about it.

This wasn't just a day of distraction. It was a day of disappearance, her from the office, her influence, her authority. She'd seen this tactic before, used against other women in finer homes with softer voices. But Mary-Ann had learned to read absence like a map: what they meant to erase revealed more than what they left in place.

The front office of Seaton Shipping was hushed when she entered. Clerks looked up, startled by her arrival.

She moved with purpose past the outer desks. A few clerks hastily stood, nodding in greeting, but their expressions were strained. One dropped his pen. Another bent quickly over his ledger, refusing to meet her eye. Their silence wasn't reverent, it was wary, as if they feared being caught in a shifting tide.

Mary-Ann's steps slowed slightly. Had Rodney spoken to them? Warned them? Or simply acted with such confidence that no one thought to question his presence? Her hand brushed the curve of her hip, steadying herself. If there were rules being rewritten, she intended to see the ink.

Her boots struck the floor harder than she intended. They echoed through the front office as she headed toward her corner office, only to halt in the doorway.

Rodney Wilkinson stood behind her desk, sleeves rolled, ledger open. He looked perfectly at ease, as though the room belonged to him. He didn't look up.

"Reviewing figures?" she asked, stepping just inside the doorway.

Rodney didn't glance up. "Someone must. The ledgers are in disarray."

"I wasn't aware they required your attention."

He closed the book with an audible snap. "Your father invited me to take a more active role."

Mary-Ann kept her voice light. "In overseeing operations?"

"In correcting them." He straightened, gazing and assessing. "It's no secret the numbers have faltered. You've done your best, I'm sure, but certain matters are better handled with experience."

A thread of tension wound tight in her spine. "I've managed them for years."

"And I've tolerated that longer than most men would." He rounded the desk slowly. "Once we're married, you'll be free of such burdens. You may focus on your proper duties."

She tilted her head slightly. "And what might those be?"

He smiled thinly. "Dressing well. Hosting teas. Bearing my name without embarrassing it. You've had your little interlude, Mary-Ann. It's time to behave like a wife."

She didn't reply, but her fingers moved toward the desk, eyes scanning the open ledger. A note in the margin caught her eye.

The ink. The shape of the g. The same slant she'd seen before.

She reached for a scrap of paper nearby, folding it in half with unhurried precision and tucking it into her glove.

His gaze flicked to her hands, and his jaw tightened. Perhaps he sensed the movement. Perhaps he only saw that she had taken something and not asked. But he said nothing, just narrowed his eyes, as if recalculating.

Rodney's smile faltered. "Is there something else?"

Her voice was calm, almost pleasant. "No. Thank you."

Something in her chest lurched, unexpected, unsteady.

At that moment, the door behind her opened. Her father stepped inside, his gaze flicking from one to the other. "Is everything in order?"

Mary-Ann turned toward him, schooling her features. "Quite. I've finished what I came to see."

"Excellent. Rodney, a word, privately, if you don't mind."

She gave a polite nod and stepped past her father.

The door had barely shut when she heard his voice, firm and cutting:

"You will never speak to my daughter that way again. Do you understand me? I built this company with my hands before you were old enough to sign your name. Mary-Ann has earned her place here. If you cannot respect that, you have no business in this office." He paused for a long heartbeat. "Or in her future. If you ever presume to belittle her again, you'll find yourself dismissed from more than polite company. Do I make myself clear?"

There was silence. Then the faint creak of a chair, and Rodney's voice, tight, forced into civility.

"Of course, sir."

But there was a crack in it. A strain that hadn't been there before.

Mr. Seaton didn't answer. The silence he left behind was far heavier than any further warning.

Outside the door, Mary-Ann paused. She hadn't meant to

linger, but something in her father's tone rooted her to the floor. Her fingers curled against her skirts. For the first time in days, she felt something shift. It wasn't a victory, but the smallest tilt in the balance.

Back at the house, Mrs. Aldridge entered Mary-Ann's room with fresh linens only to find Lydia standing near the writing desk, rifling through the drawers.

"Is there something I can help you find?" she asked, her tone clipped but pleasant.

Lydia started. "Oh, I—I was just tidying."

Mrs. Aldridge arched a brow. "In the mistress's private desk?"

Before Lydia could reply, Mr. Hollis appeared in the corridor. "Miss Lydia, you've been assigned to accompany Miss Seaton in public. Not to inspect her rooms. We do not enter without invitation."

Lydia's mouth snapped shut.

Mrs. Aldridge continued about her task, stripping the bed with methodical efficiency, but her eyes never left Lydia's form entirely. When Lydia finally retreated, spine stiff with annoyance, Mrs. Aldridge gave it another minute before moving. Then, casually, she moved to the far wall, lifted a loose panel in the wainscoting, and reached into the small recess.

She withdrew the cloth-bound booklet, her expression unreadable, and slid it between the folds of the laundry. The motion was smooth, practiced. There was no panic, only certainty. She buttoned up the bundle.

Later, once the room was quiet, Lydia slipped back inside. It took her a while, but after her diligent search, she found the loose wood. She knelt at the wall, pried open the panel, and reached inside.

Her fingers brushed a small tin box.

She pulled it free, opened the lid, and found nothing but a child's keepsakes. A button. A ribbon. A smooth stone.

Lydia's mouth pressed into a tight line. Her hand hovered over the stone as if she expected it to transform. Then she stood abruptly, brushing imaginary dust from her skirts, her movements clipped. Whatever she'd hoped to find was gone, and her failure would not go unnoticed.

Her brows drew together.

The hiding place had been used. But what she was looking for… was gone, if it was ever there. Or did someone get there first?

Chapter Twenty-Seven

THURSDAY EVENING, THE moon high and the house asleep, Mary-Ann shut the door to her bedroom and leaned against it, the weight of the morning pressing against her ribs. Her gloves were still on, though she hadn't noticed. The leather was warm now, stretched and creased at the fingers.

She peeled them off slowly, crossing to the vanity. A pitcher of fresh water stood waiting, and beside it, a folded linen bundle with a faint scent of lavender.

A knock at the door startled her.

"Come in," she called, her voice steadier than she felt.

Mrs. Aldridge stepped in, her hands tucked into the apron she always wore during morning rounds. "Thought you might need fresh towels, miss. And perhaps a moment to breathe."

Mary-Ann managed a tired smile. "You always know."

Mrs. Aldridge moved with quiet purpose, setting the bundle on the chair near the hearth. She hesitated just a moment longer than usual.

"There's more going on in this house than there ought to be," she said softly. "And some of us have eyes to see it."

Mary-Ann looked up. "Is something wrong?"

Mrs. Aldridge didn't answer right away. Instead, she opened the folded linen to reveal not towels, but a familiar cloth-wrapped booklet, the ledger she'd hidden.

Mary-Ann's breath caught. "But… it was in the wall." Mary-Ann blinked. "How did you know where to find it?"

Mrs. Aldridge's mouth curved, just barely. "Same place you hid that kitten when you were nine. The one you found behind the stables and swore to protect from your father's old hound."

Mary-Ann's lips parted. "You remember that?"

"The entire household was turning over boots and boxes looking for that poor creature. Mr. Hollis was the one who found it, curled up behind the panel, shivering and wrapped in one of your old petticoats."

A breath of laughter escaped her, soft and stunned. "I'd forgotten."

"We hadn't," Mrs. Aldridge said gently. "You've always known how to keep what matters safe." She stepped closer, her voice quiet but firm. "You trusted your instincts enough to hide it. Trust them again, miss. And know this: whatever game Mr. Wilkinson and that lady's maid are playing, not everyone in this house is fooled."

Mary-Ann reached for the booklet slowly, cradling it in both hands. She felt the shape of it, the familiar weight. Her fingers tightened. "I hadn't realized it was missing," she said quietly.

"You were never meant to," Mrs. Aldridge replied. "But someone else did."

There was a long pause. Mary-Ann looked up, emotion rising unbidden in her throat. "You knew," she said.

Mary-Ann held the book tighter.

Mrs. Aldridge patted her hand gently. "Whatever else happens, you're not alone. Not with us here." She turned and left, closing the door softly behind her.

Mary-Ann stood in place for several moments, the ledger clutched against her chest. The quiet settled around her, enveloping her, still and close, but her thoughts moved swiftly, not just about the book or what had been taken, but about the realization that she was no longer alone in this fight.

She set the ledger down gently and crossed to the window, needing some air. Just as she reached to open the windowpane, she caught movement near the gates. A familiar figure was striding up the walk, his coat dark against the green hedges.

Quinton.

He hadn't sent word ahead, hadn't asked permission. He simply came, as if drawn by some unspoken summons. Mary-Ann watched him from the window a moment longer, then turned and made her way downstairs.

She found him in the garden a few minutes later, standing near the edge of the rose arbor with his hands clasped behind his back. The breeze teased his hair, and the morning light softened the edge of his profile.

"You're early for an uninvited caller," she said lightly.

Quinton turned. The corner of his mouth tilted up. "And you're late for someone hiding a kingdom behind her wainscoting."

She arched a brow. "Wait. How do you know about the wainscoting?"

He paused, clearly caught.

"Who told you?" she pressed. "That hiding place wasn't common knowledge."

Quinton shifted, not looking away. "No one told me directly. Mrs. Aldridge mentioned that something had been recovered. She didn't say what, but I put the rest together. She said you've always known how to keep what matters safe. That sounded like you."

Mary-Ann studied him. "So you guessed."

"I remembered how you used to squirrel things away when we were younger, behind books, under loose stones, inside hollow chair legs. It made sense you'd still do it."

She tilted her head. "You always were annoyingly observant."

"And you were always impossible to surprise. I come bearing no refreshments. Only admiration."

Mary-Ann smiled, the expression unguarded. "That's new."

"I've always admired you," he said. "I just wasn't always brave enough to admit it."

Something in her chest fluttered, an ache, a memory, a

warmth she hadn't dared name.

That quieted her. For a moment, the garden was filled only with the sounds of birdsong and the faint rustling of leaves.

She stepped closer. "I'm glad you're here, but I'm also interested to know why, Quinton?"

He looked down at his hands. "Barrington sent me. He thought you might want an update on the investigation. But I think… I think I came because I wanted to see if you were all right."

Mary-Ann's breath caught, not from surprise, but from the ache in his voice. She hadn't realized how much she'd needed to hear it. She looked away for a moment, steadying herself, and studied him for a long moment. "And what exactly did Barrington tell you?"

Quinton hesitated. "Only that things were shifting. That someone needed to check the weather before the storm broke."

Mary-Ann's lips tilted faintly. "He does enjoy speaking in riddles."

A corner of Quinton's mouth twitched. "I think he hoped I'd understand yours."

She looked down at her hands, then back up. "I'm holding steady for now. But I'm beginning to feel the wind shift."

He met her eyes, and something passed between them, something familiar, fragile, and just beginning to rebuild.

"I never believed you would." His voice was low, almost reverent.

Their silence stretched again, companionable now. A breeze stirred the ivy near the garden wall.

Mary-Ann exhaled softly. "Did you ever think," she asked, "that this would be us someday? Trading truths in a garden, as if it were normal?

He didn't answer right away. His gaze lingered on hers, steady and quiet, as if choosing his words with care.

"No," he said finally. "But I'm glad it is."

He glanced toward the house, then back at her. "I should go.

I wasn't meant to stay long."

She nodded slowly, the breeze lifting a strand of hair at her temple. "Thank you…for coming."

"If there's anything you need, anything at all, send word," he said. "I'll come faster than the weather."

A smile curved her lips, small and sincere. "I'll remember that."

She wanted to reach for him, just lightly, his sleeve, his hand, anything. But instead, she stood still.

He hesitated for just a breath, then gave a slight bow. Then he was gone, striding back down the garden path the same way he had come quietly, without fanfare, but with purpose.

Mary-Ann stayed where she was, the echo of his words lingering like warmth in the air.

She didn't return to the garden bench. Instead, she stepped back inside and climbed the stairs slowly, the morning quiet settling deeper into the halls. Her room was just as she left it, sunlight streaming across the floor, the ledger still resting atop her vanity.

She reached for it with one hand, intending to tuck it away properly this time, then paused. A folded piece of paper lay atop it, worn at the edges, its parchment thinner than her own.

Her breath caught. It wasn't hers. She lifted it gently, unfolding the creases with care.

My dearest Mary-Ann,

I do not know whether this letter will reach you. Perhaps by the time it does, if it does, you will have moved on, and I would not blame you. There is no room in war for fairness, nor in fate for decency.

I write because I must. Because silence in these walls is louder than cannon fire.

There is no one here who knows your laugh. No one who would understand the way you used to speak of figures and freight as if it were poetry. No one who would think it a tri-

umph to see you walk into a counting room and make it your own.

I see you in the mornings, in the quiet before orders are shouted. I see you in the long hours when nothing moves but my thoughts. I see you before I sleep, when the dark presses in and I need a reason to hold on.

It is always you.

You are the thought that keeps me upright, the memory that steadies my hands, the future I whisper to myself when hope seems foolish.

I will love you for eternity.

—Q

Mary-Ann stood motionless, the letter trembling in her hands. She traced the edge of the parchment, thinking not only of what had reached her, but what had not. How many letters had vanished into silence? How many truths had been kept from them both?

There was no flourish, no explanation. Just his voice. Undeniably his. Left behind like a heartbeat pressed into the page.

She sat slowly on the edge of the bed, the paper still open across her palm. And for the first time in days, she let the tears come.

Later, once her breath had steadied and the letter lay carefully folded on her desk, Mary-Ann descended the stairs in search of answers. She found Mrs. Aldridge in the laundry, folding linen with practiced precision. The scent of starch and lavender lingered in the warm air.

Mary-Ann didn't speak at first. She stepped inside and held out the letter.

The housekeeper looked up, saw the paper, and paused.

"I found it inside the ledger," Mary-Ann said softly. "Did you...?"

Mrs. Aldridge wiped her hands on her apron. "It was tucked there when I retrieved the book, yes. I wasn't sure if you'd already read it or if it had been hidden."

"It hadn't," Mary-Ann said. Her fingers closed gently around the folded sheet. "Do you know where it came from?"

Mrs. Aldridge shook her head. "Only that Mr. Hollis found it among a parcel the Brigade sent over. Said it had been caught up in the mess of lost correspondence. He recognized the handwriting and thought it might be meant for you. He didn't read it, of course."

"No," Mary-Ann said quietly. "Of course."

Mrs. Aldridge looked at her for a long moment. "It matters, doesn't it?"

Mary-Ann nodded. "It changes everything."

Chapter Twenty-Eight

THE FRIDAY MORNING sun filtered through the dining room's tall windows, casting a warm glow over the silver teapot and neatly arranged toast rack. Mary-Ann stirred her tea, watching the steam curl upward, her thoughts already two steps ahead.

Her father sat at the head of the table, reading glasses perched on the bridge of his nose, a newspaper spread open before him. He hadn't said much. He rarely did the first thing in the morning, but there was a crease between his brows that hadn't been there last week.

"Father," she said softly.

He looked up. "Yes, my girl?"

She smiled faintly at the endearment. "I wondered if we might spend some time today reviewing the ledgers together. I know Mr. Wilkinson has been overseeing things, but I... I'd like to see them with you."

Mr. Seaton folded the paper slowly. "Of course. I've missed working beside you."

The words warmed her more than the tea. A memory surfaced. She was eleven years old, seated beside him at this very table with a pencil twice her size and ink smudged on her cheek. She had begged to help with the cargo manifests, only to fall asleep in the middle of the column. He'd carried her to bed and finished the work by lamplight.

She reached for a slice of toast, gathering her thoughts.

"You used to wrinkle your nose at coffee," he said suddenly, a small smile touching his mouth. "Now you take it darker than I do."

She looked at him, surprised. "I've had reasons to stay sharp lately."

He studied her for a moment, his expression thoughtful. "Good."

"Has the *Argent Wind* reported in yet?" she asked casually, referring to one of their smaller coastal ships.

He blinked, then frowned. "No, not yet. It's a day or two behind, but nothing unusual—not this early in the spring."

"Still," she said gently, "you've always told me a good captain sends word ahead."

"I did say that, didn't I?" He sighed and reached for his coffee. Barrington mentioned it yesterday, as a matter of fact. He said he might have someone look into it, just to be cautious.

Mary-Ann raised her brows slightly. "Who?"

"I didn't ask. Likely one of his men or Quinton, perhaps. He said someone was heading to Scarborough."

She nodded, absorbing the information. So Barrington was already investigating.

"I'll make time this afternoon for the ledgers," her father said, his voice gentler now. "Just like old times?"

"Just like," she echoed.

And for the first time in days, the tension in her shoulders eased a fraction. The balance was shifting subtly, but real. She could feel it in the air, as surely as the scent of toast and tea.

Mary-Ann was not halfway up the stairs when Lydia appeared at the landing, hands clasped, smile fixed.

"Miss Seaton," she said brightly, "I thought perhaps a drive to the park this morning? The air is lovely, and Mr. Wilkinson said it would be good for your nerves."

Mary-Ann paused two steps from the top. "My nerves are quite sound, thank you."

Lydia's smile flickered. "Well, a change of scenery—"

"—would interfere with my schedule," Mary-Ann said pleasantly. "But I'm sure you'll find something else to occupy yourself."

A flash of something passed behind Lydia's eyes, irritation, perhaps, or calculation.

"Very good, miss."

But she didn't move. Instead, Lydia offered a smile that didn't reach her eyes.

"You won't have to worry about managing a house once you're married," she added smoothly. "I'll be there."

Mary-Ann stopped short, blinking.

Lydia's expression turned smug. "Mr. Wilkinson has hired me as the housekeeper in his new home. I thought I ought to get accustomed to the rhythm of things."

Mary-Ann said nothing. Not yet. But her smile returned, calm and unreadable.

So that was the game. Not a companion, but a shadow in silk. A presence that slipped in too easily and watched too closely.

Mary-Ann continued, her steps unhurried. Behind her, she could hear Lydia descending the stairs, the sound just a bit too sharp.

She had nearly reached the hall when the drawing room door flew open.

"There you are!" Mrs. Bainbridge swept in, trailing a bolt of ivory ribbon and a folded invitation. "You must come help me. A baron's nephew is now refusing to sit beside a viscount's daughter, and I've been told the cake baker is threatening to elope with the florist."

Mary-Ann blinked. "Is that… figurative?"

"Not even slightly," Bainbridge said. "They've taken a chaise and three bottles of champagne and are nowhere to be found."

Mary-Ann clapped her hand over her mouth. Had she just laughed? Out loud? She hadn't expected to find a moment of absurdity tucked between suspicion and worry, but Mrs. Bainbridge always managed it. "Come," Bainbridge said, linking their arms. "We'll rescue the guest list, restore order to the ribbons, and pretend your lady's maid isn't sulking like a slighted governess."

Mary-Ann allowed herself to be swept along. Tuesday mornings with Mrs. Bainbridge had become a welcome routine, even if they sometimes came with ribbons and minor noble chaos. For now.

They were halfway through arranging seating cards by rank, reputation, and likelihood of political offense when Hollis stepped discreetly into the room.

"Begging your pardon, Miss Seaton," he said to Mary-Ann. "Mr. Kenworth is in the front hall. He asks for a moment of your time."

Mrs. Bainbridge immediately perked up. "Barrington's man? Oh, do ask if he has strong feelings about lavender. These ribbons are destroying my will to live."

Mary-Ann rose, brushing a smudge of ink from her sleeve. "I'll return shortly."

Before she could leave the room, Mrs. Bainbridge stood as well, gathering her scattered papers and bits of ribbon. "Oh, have him help me carry these things, would you? I can't manage the guest list and my dignity at the same time. My house is close to Barrington's. I won't take him out of his way."

Kenworth stood just inside the door, gloved hands neatly folded behind his back. He bowed when she entered.

"Miss Seaton. His lordship sends his regards. I've been asked to deliver a few updates."

She nodded. "Go on."

Your father's vessel, the *Argent Wind,* has not yet arrived at port in Scarborough. Lord Barrington has dispatched Captain Hollingsworth to investigate more closely. He departed at first light."

Mary-Ann's breath caught, not in pain, but with the surprise of a shift in the wind. She imagined saying goodbye at the garden gate, offering caution in place of care. Instead, he had simply gone. It was a reasonable silence. And it stung anyway.

"He's in Scarborough?"

"Yes, my lady. Lord Barrington believed he was best suited to the task. A discreet hand, loyal eyes."

She folded her arms, more to keep her balance than to appear unimpressed. "He didn't think to tell me himself?"

Kenworth's mouth twitched faintly. "He may have wished to. But dawn does not always allow for courtesies."

She nodded once. "Thank you."

She told herself it didn't matter, that the work came first, that it always had. But her hand tightened slightly against her sleeve. He should have told her.

She hadn't realized how much she'd been hoping to see him. Just once more, before this all began.

Kenworth inclined his head again. "If there is anything you wish to relay to his lordship or the captain, you need only send word."

"I will."

She turned, but Kenworth added quietly, "Captain Hollingsworth left with a purpose. That's usually when he does his best work."

Mary-Ann paused, then offered a small smile. "So do I."

The house was quiet again. Mary-Ann returned to her room without interruption, her mind already stitching together pieces of a plan. She moved with purpose now, not the hesitant caution of days past, but with the calm certainty of someone who had decided which truths to pursue.

She crossed to her writing desk and sat, listening to the hush of the room, the faint creak of floorboards beneath her chair, the whisper of the sea beyond the glass. She didn't write a letter. She made a list.

- Wilkinson's control at the docks
- The altered ledger
- The missing *Argent Wind*

- Lydia's probing questions
- The recovered letter

She stared at the list, letting the shape of it settle in her mind. It wasn't just a trail. It was a map. And the more she looked, the more it seemed to point to a single destination: the docks. It was no longer a collection of strange events. It was a pattern.

She folded the page and tucked it behind a dull household note in the journal, then slipped it into the back of a drawer. A record for herself. A thread to follow later when no one else was watching.

She passed the desk on her way to the wardrobe, her gaze brushing the corner where the letter still lay. She hadn't touched it since the first reading. She didn't need to. Its words had rooted beneath her skin, steadying her every step since.

She rose and crossed to the wardrobe, choosing a sensible cloak, sturdy boots, and a reticule containing coins and gloves. It was time to return to the docks. But this time, she wouldn't be following breadcrumbs. She'd be leaving them.

Chapter Twenty-Nine

FRIDAY EVENING, THE smell of salt and tar wrapped around Mary-Ann the moment she stepped off the carriage near the warehouse offices. The wind off the water was brisk, tugging at the edge of her cloak and stirring the hem of her skirts. It wasn't quite noon, and yet the harbor buzzed with movement. Sailors called across rigging, crates creaked on pulleys, and dockhands shouted to one another above the churn of tide and trade.

It looked like order. It smelled like business. But Mary-Ann no longer trusted appearances. She held a folded sheet of shipping records in her hand, a legitimate errand in case anyone questioned her presence. She'd taken care to choose a day when she knew Wilkinson would be at the Guild meeting in Newcastle.

Inside the warehouse office, the bookkeeper barely looked up when she entered.

"Morning, Miss Seaton. Didn't expect you today."

"I needed to clarify a discrepancy," she said, setting the folded paper on the edge of his desk. "Cargo weights on the *Branford Belle* don't match the manifest totals."

He frowned, pulling the paper toward him. "Likely a copying error, but I'll double-check it."

She nodded, her tone polite, then drifted toward the far wall of ledgers as if browsing.

Two voices murmured beyond the partition. Men were speaking in hushed tones, too faint for words, but the cadence was sharp. She tilted her head subtly, pretending to examine the spine of a leather-bound log.

"…wasn't meant to dock again so soon," one said.

"…barely cleaned out from the last run." The second voice cursed under his breath.

A hinge creaked. Mary-Ann moved swiftly, taking the nearest ledger off the shelf and flipping it open.

One of the men stepped into view a moment later, wiping his hands on a cloth. He paused when he saw her.

"Miss Seaton," he said, startled. "Didn't know you were here."

"Just reviewing a few entries," she said, turning a page.

He nodded, slow and wary. "Everything in order?"

"For now."

He gave a brief nod and disappeared through the side door, heading toward the loading dock.

Mary-Ann replaced the ledger and returned to the desk. "Thank you for your help. I'll return the report once I've gone over it again."

The clerk gave a vague grunt.

She stepped back out into the wind, her mind racing. A ship that wasn't supposed to dock again. A last run that had to be "cleaned out." And no record of it anywhere on the manifest.

She followed the curve of the harbor wall slowly, her eyes scanning the names of moored ships. *Branford Belle. Argent Wind.* The latter bobbed faintly in its berth, despite being supposedly overdue. She knew its usual captain kept to a strict calendar, never idle in port without cause.

Something was very wrong. And someone was lying. She turned back toward the carriage, eyes narrowed against the light. Let them think she'd come to chase numbers. She was chasing something far more dangerous.

By the time Mary-Ann arrived home, the clouds had thickened, and the light coming through the drawing room windows had cooled to a pale gray. She'd barely removed her gloves when Lydia appeared in the hall, her expression all composed concern.

"There you are," she said lightly, stepping forward. "I was beginning to worry."

Mary-Ann handed her gloves to Hollis, who took them with a quiet nod. "No need."

"I thought you'd gone to the seamstress." Lydia's tone was pleasant, but there was a faint edge beneath it.

"Plans changed."

Lydia followed her into the drawing room like a shadow, her footsteps muffled against the carpet. "I do hope you weren't out alone. Mr. Wilkinson's been quite clear about keeping a proper escort."

Mary-Ann turned slowly, her smile cool. "And yet I wasn't aware Mr. Wilkinson had been promoted to Lord Chancellor."

Lydia blinked at the rebuke, then recovered quickly. "Only meant for your protection, of course."

"Of course."

A pause stretched between them, thin and brittle.

"You'll want to be mindful of such things," Lydia continued, straightening a vase on the nearby table with casual precision. "It won't be long before this house is no longer your concern."

Mary-Ann lifted a brow. "Oh?"

Lydia's smile stretched. "I did mention it the other day. Mr. Wilkinson has offered me a permanent position. A housekeeper, of course. But with my knowledge of your habits, it only makes sense."

Mary-Ann felt it then, a flicker of heat in her chest, slow and steady. She stared at Lydia for a long moment, letting the silence stretch. Then, lightly: "And you accepted?"

Lydia's smile didn't waver. "It's all but settled."

Mary-Ann stepped forward and reached for the tea tray. "Shall I pour, or would you prefer to continue implying my life has already been decided for me?"

Lydia didn't answer. But the smugness in her expression said enough.

Mary-Ann handed her a cup. "Careful. It's hot." Let her think she'd won. It would make what came next all the more satisfying.

The front door slammed open not a moment later, followed by a flurry of skirts, raised voices, and what sounded suspiciously like a tangle of hatboxes.

"Oh, blast the walkway stones. Hollis, do be a dear and rescue the lilac ribbons before they scatter to Kent!"

Mary-Ann turned just in time to see Mrs. Bainbridge sweep into the drawing room, cheeks flushed, gloves mismatched, and hair only half-pinned. A feather stuck out at an angle that suggested war rather than fashion.

"Why is it always windy when I need serenity?" she demanded, then paused upon seeing Lydia. Her expression brightened with dramatic delight. "Miss Lydia! What a surprise. I hadn't realized today was your turn to hover."

Mary-Ann blinked. There was a bite beneath Bainbridge's sweetness she hadn't heard before. It was cool, practiced, and unmistakably deliberate.

Lydia's mouth thinned. "I was merely serving tea."

"Splendid. Serve it elsewhere."

Lydia hesitated.

Mary-Ann gestured without looking. "That will be all, Miss Finch."

With a stiff curtsy, Lydia vanished. Refined or not, Mrs. Bainbridge wielded her words like scalpels when she chose. And today was one of those days.

Bainbridge collapsed onto the settee with a groan, kicking off one shoe. "Honestly, between your father's dreadful penmanship and my cousin's duel over a dessert fork, I may call off the wedding and elope with my own dog."

Mary-Ann bit back a smile. "I imagine he would object."

"He'd be honored. He listens when I speak."

Then, with a sigh and more gravity, Bainbridge added, "I saw something odd this morning. I wasn't going to mention it, but now… I think I must."

Mary-Ann's smile faded. "What did you see?"

"I was in the fish market, don't ask, and I saw your lady's maid. Lydia. Near the docks. She wasn't shopping. She was standing behind the fishmonger's stall, staring out at the harbor as if memorizing the tides.

Mary-Ann's spine went still.

"She didn't see me," Bainbridge added. "But it didn't look like an errand."

"No," Mary-Ann murmured. "It wouldn't."

Bainbridge leaned forward, tone quieter. "I don't suppose there's anything you'd like to tell me?"

Mary-Ann met her gaze steadily. "Yes. But not here."

They relocated to Mary-Ann's bedroom under the pretense of selecting a shawl from her wardrobe. Hollis offered to bring tea, and Bainbridge distracted him with a fabricated crisis involving crushed invitation seals. Once the door was shut behind them, the mood shifted.

Mary-Ann turned the key in the lock and leaned back against the door. "I need you to listen and not dismiss what I'm about to say."

Mrs. Bainbridge lowered herself into the armchair near the window, her tone losing its usual lilt. "I'm listening."

Mary-Ann didn't pace. She crossed to her writing desk and opened the drawer slowly, drawing out the folded list she'd written the night before.

"This is what I know or suspect. Wilkinson is manipulating the shipping accounts. The *Argent Wind* was listed as missing, but I saw it at the docks today. Men are speaking in hushed tones, cargo is unrecorded, and I found altered ledgers in my father's study. Lydia's placement here wasn't for my comfort. It was surveillance."

She passed the page to Mrs. Bainbridge, who read it in silence.

When she looked up, her face was pale, but resolute. "You're not being paranoid."

"No," Mary-Ann said. "I'm being followed. And now I'm following back."

Bainbridge folded the list with care. "What are you going to do?"

"There's one place left to search. The sea cave."

"The one from the newspaper?"

Mary-Ann nodded. "If anything is still hidden, it's there. And I can't wait for Quinton. I don't know when he'll be back or what he's allowed to tell me. But if I could choose, I would rather not do this without him."

Bainbridge didn't argue. She only asked, "Do you want me to come with you?"

Mary-Ann hesitated. "No. I need you to go to Barrington. Tell him what I've told you. Tell him where I've gone. But don't come after me unless I fail to return."

Bainbridge rose, straightening her spine like a soldier receiving orders. "Then we both have something to do."

Mary-Ann reached for her cloak, fingers firm on the fabric.

"If I'm wrong, they'll mock my pride. But if I'm right... Someone has twisted my family's name into a shield for corruption. And I will not let that stand.

Chapter Thirty

S UNDAY MORNING, AFTER a restless night, Mary-Ann sat at the breakfast table, smoothing her napkin across her lap, her expression perfectly composed as Lydia prattled on about linens. The breakfast table was set with precision, marmalade in a cut-glass dish, eggs gone slightly cold, and tea she hadn't tasted. Her father sat at the head of the table, more tired than usual, though he made an effort to murmur polite responses now and then.

"I do think the pale green would suit the dining room better, don't you?" Lydia was saying. "It's soothing. And it reflects the light in a very forgiving way."

Mary-Ann nodded. "Lovely."

Lydia beamed. "Of course, Mr. Wilkinson has excellent taste. He said we should embrace the modern hues. He's ordered new wallpaper samples to arrive next week."

Across the table, Mr. Seaton's fork paused mid-air.

Mary-Ann folded a slice of toast neatly on her plate. "How efficient of him. I had no idea wallpaper was among his many talents."

"Oh, he's been involved in every decision." Lydia poured herself more tea. "He says you have so much on your mind, you need someone to carry the burden."

Mary-Ann looked up and smiled sweetly. "And how generous of him to volunteer you."

Her father cleared his throat. "Perhaps some matters might wait until after the wedding."

"Oh, of course, sir," Lydia said quickly. "I only meant to ease things in the meantime."

"I find things rather orderly already," Mary-Ann murmured, rising from her seat. "But you're very kind."

She crossed the room to retrieve a folded sheet from the sideboard, yesterday's cargo schedule. "Father, may I speak to you a moment before you head into town?"

He blinked. "Certainly, my girl."

Lydia rose as well, but Mary-Ann's glance over her shoulder was polite steel. "Alone, if you please."

Something in her voice, cool, clipped, certain, made even Lydia pause.

Lydia hesitated, then offered a thin smile. "Of course."

Mary-Ann led her father into the study and closed the door behind them. The ledger she'd left on the desk the night before was undisturbed. She laid the cargo schedule beside it.

"I noticed a conflict between the inventory log and the dock reports," she said. "The *Maribel* was offloaded two days ago, but the manifest says she hasn't made port."

Her father frowned, adjusting his spectacles. "That can't be right. We would've received confirmation."

"We didn't. But she's on the books at the harbor office."

He scratched his chin. "Wilkinson told me the *Maribel* was delayed in the north."

Mary-Ann met his gaze. "Then either the harbor's lying, or Wilkinson is."

A silence hung between them, one that said more than words. For the first time, she wasn't seeking his approval. She was offering him the truth.

He didn't speak for a long moment. Then he folded the schedule in half. "Leave this with me. I'll look into it personally."

Mary-Ann nodded. "Thank you."

And for the first time, she saw something flicker behind her father's eyes. Not fatigue. Not confusion. Resolve.

LATER THAT MORNING, Mary-Ann slipped away from the front rooms under the pretense of inspecting a fresh delivery of linens. Lydia, still discussing drapery options with the upstairs maid, scarcely noticed.

She took the long corridor toward the rear of the house, where the morning sun filtered through narrow windows and the scent of lemon oil lingered faintly in the air. Mrs. Aldridge was just finishing with the silver chest when she looked up.

"Miss," she said quietly, straightening. "Might I have a word?"

Mary-Ann nodded, stepping into the butler's pantry. It was dim and narrow, tucked between service rooms, and a place of quiet and secrets.

Mrs. Aldridge reached into her apron and pulled out a folded envelope. "I found this yesterday. Behind the small table in the front hall. It was meant for you."

Mary-Ann opened it. The handwriting was unfamiliar, but the contents were clear: a merchant's note, confirming a delivery she had never received. Dated nearly three weeks prior. Her name was on the front. Her father's seal was beneath.

Mrs. Aldridge had quietly handed her a folded slip of paper with Mr. Hollis's neat script listing the merchant's response. A pearl-handled dressing case, monogrammed combs included, ordered in Mr. Seaton's name and delivered not to their home, but to a lodging house off Cavendish Street. Lydia had signed for it.

Mary-Ann read it twice more, then folded it again and tucked it into her glove.

"Thank you," she said. "You did exactly right."

She turned to leave but paused. "Mrs. Aldridge… has anyone else been asking about me? Among the staff?"

The housekeeper's mouth tightened. "Only Miss Lydia. She often asks about your schedule. And once, about the lock on your writing desk."

Mary-Ann absorbed that in silence.

"I've reminded the staff that such questions are not to be answered," Mrs. Aldridge added.

Mary-Ann met her gaze. "Thank you. Please continue to do so."

She stepped out into the corridor again, her pace slower now, her thoughts sharper.

Intercepted letters. Watching eyes. And now a desk lock that Lydia had no business wondering about.

Whatever Rodney Wilkinson was planning, he hadn't expected her to be paying attention. And that was his first mistake.

BY EARLY AFTERNOON, Mary-Ann found herself once again inside the Seaton offices near the quay. She had claimed a need to fetch archived documents for wedding accounting, a believable excuse that kept Lydia at bay.

The office smelled of ink and dust, the windows thrown open to the salt-heavy breeze. Ledgers stretched across the back wall in orderly rows, a familiar rhythm from childhood days when she'd curled beside her father to practice sums and sea routes. But now, there was little comfort in the neat columns.

She set down her reticule and reached for the shipping records dated two weeks prior. The pages were crisply folded, too crisp. New parchment tucked into old bindings.

Her finger traced the entry for the *Maribel*. The cargo weight was listed as standard. So was the destination. But the departure port… had changed.

She flipped backward through earlier entries. The *Maribel* had always departed from Branscombe Dock. But now it claimed Northgate Port.

Mary-Ann frowned. Northgate was nearly forty miles inland.

No one with any knowledge of tides and drafts would send a vessel of the *Maribel's* size there.

A sound behind her made her still. Boots on stone. Not heavy enough to be her father. Not light enough to be Kenworth.

She turned, ledger still open in her hands.

A junior clerk she didn't recognize offered a quick bow. "Apologies, miss. I didn't know anyone was in here."

She forced a smile. "Just reviewing accounts. My father asked me to double-check a few details."

"Of course. Please let me know if you need anything."

He ducked out again.

Mary-Ann didn't move. Her pulse remained high, her thoughts running faster than her breath. Another pair of eyes. Another coincidence that didn't feel like one.

She returned the ledger to its shelf and took another, scanning the recent arrivals. *Branford Belle. Argent Wind. Fallowmoor.*

She traced a line to a cargo number she recognized. It was listed under the name "R. W. Holdings." Wilkinson's initials.

Her jaw tightened. She copied the line onto a slip of paper and tucked it into her sleeve. She wasn't done yet. But she was getting close.

MARY-ANN RETURNED HOME just before sunset, her skirts tugged by the breeze and the faint scent of salt clinging to her gloves. The house was oddly quiet, the usual hum of staff movements subdued. She had just handed her shawl to Hollis when she heard a knock at the front door.

Hollis opened it. "Captain Hollingsworth, sir."

Mary-Ann's breath caught, not in shock, but in something softer, something unsettled. She stepped forward before she could think better of it.

Quinton stood in the entry, travel-worn but composed, his

hair wind-ruffled and boots still dusty. He looked at her like he'd been hoping to for days.

"I've just come from Scarborough," he said. "There's news."

She stepped aside to let him in, nodding once. "Come into the drawing room."

The fire was low, barely more than embers, but she didn't call for more coals.

They sat across from each other, the silence stretching between them.

Mary-Ann didn't ask him to explain. Not at first. Instead, she stood and crossed the room to a small table beside the bookshelf. From beneath a stack of folded reports, she drew a slip of paper and handed it to him.

A symbol was scrawled in the corner, a black raven stamped onto the back of a shipping invoice.

Quinton went still. Not surprised. Not confused. Resigned.

"You know what this is," she said.

He didn't deny it. "Yes."

"What does it mean?"

He hesitated.

"Tell me, Quinton."

His jaw tightened. "It's the mark of the Order of Shadows. A syndicate that has been operating through ports and politics for decades. Maybe longer."

She stared at him. The air between them seemed to constrict.

"You've known," she said. "Since when?"

"Since just after I returned," he admitted. "Barrington briefed me on it. But I'd heard whispers, even before—"

She flinched like he'd struck her. "And you said nothing."

"I couldn't. It's not just dangerous, Mary-Ann. It's a web. A world of its own."

Her voice broke. "I asked you to trust me. I trusted *you* even when I shouldn't have. Even when you walked into my house like a ghost and gave me nothing but riddles."

"I was trying to protect you."

Her hands were trembling now. "I have walked into warehouses alone. I've had my room searched, my letters intercepted, my life rearranged. And I did it all thinking I had no one. No allies. No truth."

Quinton stood, but she rose with him, her eyes bright with tears she refused to shed.

"You let me carry it alone," she said, her voice hoarse. "You knew what Rodney was. You knew what I was walking into, and you let me believe it was just my imagination."

"I was trying to find a way to stop it without putting you at risk."

"No," she whispered. "You were trying to find a way to stop it without needing me."

His shoulders dropped. "That's not fair."

"But it's true."

She turned away, pressing a hand against the mantel as if to steady herself. She didn't want to cry. Not now. Not when her clarity had finally sharpened into something usable.

"I loved you," she said. "I never stopped. I held onto you for three years, through silence, through grief, through hope. And when you came back, I thought I had been given a second chance. But I wasn't. I was given a shadow. A man who looked like you but didn't know who I was anymore."

He crossed the room. "I do know—"

"No, you don't," she said, pulling away. "Because if you had, you would have come to me with the truth. Not when it was safe. But when it mattered."

"Mary-Ann," he said her name softly, but she shook her head.

"You don't get to call me that right now."

The silence that followed was unbearable.

Finally, she stepped to the door and opened it, her voice was a low ache. "Please go."

"Mary-Ann—"

She looked at him, one last time. "You made me feel like I was too much to love *and* too fragile to trust. That's not love.

That's control."

She hesitated, then added, more quietly, "That's what Rodney does. He makes choices for me, then calls it care. Are you really any different?"

Quinton's eyes darkened. "You can't marry him."

Mary-Ann didn't flinch. "No? Then who else is left to choose me?"

He stepped forward, but she stopped him with a look that was clear, wounded, and resolute.

"Good-bye, Captain," she said.

And when the latch clicked closed behind him, she didn't move. Not right away. The silence was hers now, and for the first time, it didn't feel like peace. It felt like an absence echoing through the room like the final click of a door left open too long.

Chapter Thirty-One

SUNDAY AFTERNOON, THE wind had shifted, bringing with it a strange urgency. The tea tray was perfect. Too perfect. The china gleamed, polished to a shine so fine it caught the firelight. The biscuits were still warm. Mary-Ann poured with steady hands, her movements graceful, practiced, like a woman untouched by grief or betrayal.

Mrs. Bainbridge noticed. She noticed everything.

"You've gone quiet," she said, accepting the cup Mary-Ann handed her. "That always used to worry me."

Mary-Ann smiled faintly. "No need to worry. It's just tea."

"Darling, if I believed that, I'd be wearing my yellow bonnet and not my walking boots."

Mary-Ann took her own seat, her back straight. "I'm fine."

"Of course you are," Mrs. Bainbridge said lightly. "Because the man you grieved for three years came back, and instead of holding you, he handed you silence. That would make anyone feel whole again."

The cup in Mary-Ann's hand trembled.

She set it down. Slowly. Deliberately. And then she said, voice barely above a whisper, "He knew."

Mrs. Bainbridge blinked. "Quinton?"

Mary-Ann nodded. "About everything. About the shipments. The symbol. The Order."

Mrs. Bainbridge's teacup clinked against its saucer as her hand trembled. "Oh my God."

"I showed him the mark I found. I asked him what it meant." Her voice was calm. Detached. *Too* detached. "He told me it wasn't safe to share. That Barrington had said—"

Mrs. Bainbridge didn't move. Didn't breathe.

"He said it wasn't about trust," Mary-Ann continued, "but that's all it has ever been about. And he failed it. I let myself believe I was safe with him," she whispered. "Even after everything. Even after he looked right through me that first day, I told myself he'd come back to me. That he'd remember who we were. But he never did."

Her eyes filled with tears, sudden and sharp, and she pressed her lips together tightly.

"I've had my privacy stripped away. My mail tampered with. My room searched. Every time I think I've clawed my way back to control, someone takes it from me."

She turned her face away for a moment, blinking furiously, but a tear slipped free despite her will. She caught it with the back of her hand and took a breath so shallow it barely stirred her chest.

Mrs. Bainbridge's voice was soft now. "My dear girl…"

"And no one does anything!" Mary-Ann said, voice rising. "They *know*. My father. Barrington. Quinton. Everyone's circling this threat like it's a fire they're afraid to smother. But it's burning through my family. Through our business. Through me."

She stood. Her chest rose and fell, her breath shallow and uneven. "My mother would have never stood for this," she said, the words escaping before she could temper them. "She would have made them answer for it."

Mrs. Bainbridge rose too, her expression shifting as grief transformed into fury.

"I won't stand by while Wilkinson turns my father into a puppet and calls it business. I won't pretend I don't see what he's doing. If no one else will stop him—" Her voice cracked, but she forced it through. "—then I will. I'll get the proof I need if I have to go into the cave and retrieve it myself.

A beat of silence passed between them.

Then Mrs. Bainbridge said, with no theatricality at all, "You are the bravest woman I know."

Her pulse thundered, but her spine held straight. She wasn't her mother's shadow. She was her echo, sharpened by grief and grown by truth. If the men couldn't bring down the Order, she would. If no one else would protect her family's name, she'd do it herself.

Mary-Ann laughed bitterly. "I'm exhausted."

"I know. And I don't blame you for what you want to do. But I'm asking you to wait until you can think clearly. As you said yourself, you're exhausted."

"I don't want to wait. But I will. For now."

Mrs. Bainbridge crossed the room and took her hands. "You have nothing to prove. Not to them. Not to anyone. But if you *must*, let me speak first. Let me try."

Mary-Ann nodded once. Her voice was barely audible. "Very well."

Mrs. Bainbridge lingered for a moment, her grip firm. "I've seen what happens to women who speak the truth too soon. I've watched wives lose their reputations for asking the wrong questions. I've seen daughters disinherited for daring to see too clearly. And you, God help them, you see everything. You ask for answers from men who think silence is safer. I won't let that be your end."

⇻⇻⇺⇺

BARRINGTON LEANED BACK in his chair, one brow lifted. "So you're saying the second ship wasn't registered under its original name?"

"No," Quinton said. "It was renamed and moved through Scarborough's south inlet. Someone's forged at least three manifests."

"The *Argent Wind*?"

"Still docked. But the markings are gone. She's being repaint-ed."

Barrington's jaw tightened. "They're preparing to disappear."

Quinton nodded, the motion sharp. "And if they succeed, we lose any hope of proving the connection." He sat without saying a word. After a long pause, he glanced at Barrington. "And we leave Seaton with a broken company and the primary suspect in smuggling."

He didn't say her name. He didn't have to.

Barrington noticed the silence. "You did the right thing, you know. Not telling her about any of this."

Quinton's gaze didn't leave the fire. "Did I?"

"She would've been a target."

"She already *was*," Quinton snapped. "You gave me an order to protect her by shutting her out. You told me to stand back and watch while she unraveled everything on her own.

Barrington looked away, and for a fleeting moment, Quinton thought he saw regret. Maybe he'd honestly believed he was shielding her. Playing the long game. But in doing so, he'd underestimated not just her abilities, but her heart. He hadn't counted on Quinton falling in love with her all over again, or on Mary-Ann seeing the cracks in their entire foundation.

"I followed that order." Quinton lifted his chin to his former commanding officer. "But not every order is right."

Barrington didn't speak.

Quinton had watched her gather herself from grief, step back into her father's house like a woman determined to build something lasting, and he hadn't trusted her with the truth. Not because she wasn't capable. But because some foolish, broken part of him still believed silence could shield her. That part of him had been wrong.

"I should've changed your mind," Quinton said. "You're a fair man. You would have listened."

He had followed orders through war, through captivity. But this one. This silence had never sat right. And now, too late, he saw what it had cost.

The fire snapped. Neither man moved. The silence between them stretched taut.

The door burst open. A gust of wind followed Mrs. Bainbridge in.

She didn't wait to be invited. She swept in like a storm, skirts snapping, eyes alight with fury. She had warned them. She had begged them to take Mary-Ann seriously. But no. Secrets were safer than trust. Orders were easier than respect. And now? Now they were chasing the consequences of their own arrogance.

"You," she said to Barrington, "are a pompous, calculating man. And you," she turned to Quinton, "are a coward."

They both stared.

"Do you know what she's done in your silence?" she said, storming into the room. "She's tracked every ship. She's copied the ledgers. Confirmed every manifest. She's confronted her father. And what have you two done? *Strategized.*"

"Honoria—"

"No, don't you *dare, Honoria me, Reese Barrington*. She told me everything. The missing ships. The raven seal. The dock names. Even the recipients. I have them written down, if your clever minds are still catching up."

Quinton stood slowly. "She found the recipient logs?"

"She found *everything*. And she's been alone in it because both of you thought keeping her in the dark and at Wilkinson's mercy was protection."

Barrington's voice turned hard. "We couldn't risk a leak."

"She *isn't* a leak. She's your best chance. She expected to be treated like a partner, not a problem. She's smarter than both of you and braver than either of you. And now you've lost her."

Quinton's jaw clenched. "Where is she?"

Mrs. Bainbridge hesitated. "At home. I think I talked her down. She said she was going to the cave, to look for proof."

Quinton went still.

The room did too.

"She wouldn't," Barrington said.

"She would," Quinton answered, already reaching for his coat. "If she believes there's proof there, nothing will stop her."

"You don't know that—"

"I do," Quinton said. His voice was low. Unshakable.

"Because I know what she looks like when she's made up her mind. And I will not let her walk into that place alone."

He crossed the room in three strides.

"She will get her proof," he said as he pulled open the door, "and if I have to die to protect her while she does, then so be it."

He paused at the threshold, turning back to Barrington one last time. His voice dropped to something dangerous, steady.

"If anything happens to her, there won't be a strategy clever enough to save you from me."

Chapter Thirty-Two

MONDAY MORNING, WITH the tide turning and shadows thick on the wharf, the records whispered what no one would say aloud.

Mary-Ann sat at her desk, the lamplight trembling over the cloth-bound booklet. She hadn't meant to linger over it, but her thumb had found the smudge near the margin, a dark streak cutting through the number eight. And just like that, she remembered.

You always missed the eights... She heard his voice. Hamish. *Ink on your nose, little miss.*

Her breath caught, and then released all at once, as certainty lit behind her eyes.

"Hamish," she whispered, a laugh breaking through the wetness in her throat. "You clever, clever man. It wasn't a farewell. Not a comfort. It was a breadcrumb."

The old warehouse. Not the one everyone used. The other one behind the ropeworks where they'd played when she was small, while her father spoke to the dockworkers. Where he taught her her first figures. Where he'd tucked sweets behind tally books and smiled every time she found them.

She rose, the chair legs whispering across the floor. Her heart beat fast, not with fear, but with purpose.

"Thank you," she said aloud, voice catching.

She crossed the room, pulling open the drawer where her gloves and scarf waited. No cloak. She needed her hands free.

The house was still. The morning air tasted of salt and promise. And for the first time in days, she felt alive. Downstairs, she paused only to retrieve the lantern from the side cupboard, the one she'd used on evening rounds with her father as a girl. She lifted it from its hook near the kitchen hearth and slid the cover to the side. The flame, still burning low, brightened just enough to light her way.

Outside, the wind had stilled. The streets were empty as she walked, slipping through back lanes and narrow alleys toward the old warehouse near the water. It had once been part of the Seaton holdings, decommissioned years ago, too remote and too weather-worn for regular use. And yet...

Mary-Ann slipped the ring of keys from her pocket, the brass cool and familiar. Her fingers paused on the worn leather strap. She remembered the day her father handed her the keys, his pride, her solemn promise. She hadn't known then just how much that promise would demand. The lock gave with a groan. The door swung inward. She stepped inside.

Dust and cold greeted her like old memories. The air inside the warehouse was thick with the scent of salt, oil, and wood long left to rot. Mary-Ann held the lantern higher, its glow pushing back the shadows only a few feet in each direction.

Crates lined the walls. Some were empty, and some were marked with dates that didn't match any recent ledgers. She stepped carefully, her footsteps echoing in the cavernous stillness.

One stack near the back caught her eye. It bore the Seaton Shipping seal, but an older version, retired years ago. The wax was brittle, the wood warped. As she knelt to examine it, her hand brushed something wedged between the crate and the wall.

A folio. Leather-bound, weathered, sealed with a red ribbon now fraying at the edges. There was no label on the outside, only a faint impression of SS *Seaton Shipping*, pressed in gold leaf and nearly worn away.

Her breath caught. She opened it. She turned another page, careful with the frayed ribbon, and something fluttered loose—no ledger, no receipt, just a small, folded note. Her breath caught.

It was Hamish's handwriting. Familiar. Steady.

I knew you would find this. Keep it safe. — H.

Her throat tightened, and for a single, aching moment, everything in her stilled. "Thank you," she whispered, and tucked the note gently back inside.

She turned the next page and found page after page of meticulous records, including ship names, arrival dates, and aliases. Notes in shorthand and ink-smudged sketches of symbols, ravens, ciphers, and foreign ports. A different ledger was tucked within manifest entries tied to Seaton vessels but routed through false ports. Half the names had been removed from Seaton's official books.

And then, in the center, tucked between two thicker sheets, a page of diagrams.

Not cargo. Not routes. People.

Mary-Ann's hand trembled as she lifted it. It was a personnel chart, neat and chilling. One name stood at the top. Rodney Wilkinson.

Lines stretched out from his name. Some to merchant houses, others to warehouse supervisors. But at the base was a box that made her blood run cold.

Mary-Ann Seaton.

Beside it: Contract pending. Consolidation of Seaton Shipping is imminent.

Her knees nearly gave out. She steadied herself on the crate. The warehouse tilted slightly, or maybe it was her knees. Her future, her family, her love, all reduced to ink on a page. Her name, written not as a daughter, not as an heiress, but as an acquisition. A line on a chart. A means to power. They hadn't just used her company. They had tried to use *her*.

This wasn't business. It wasn't smuggling. It was a takeover. A quiet, calculated invasion of her father's company. And

Quinton—

Her heart stuttered.

Quinton's name wasn't on the page at all. Because he wasn't meant to be part of their future, he'd been erased.

Beneath the chart, tucked behind a slip of blotting paper, was a report. No heading. No signature. Just a chilling summary in clean, decisive hand:

Interference removed. Operation successful. Hollingsworth detained as intended. Seaton interest remains vulnerable, consolidation imminent. Wilkinson's position secured with minimal resistance.

Her vision blurred. She read the words again, barely able to breathe. They hadn't just wanted to ruin the company. They'd orchestrated Quinton's capture, not as the cost of war, but as its strategy. A calculated removal. He hadn't been collateral. He had been the first move.

Mary-Ann stood slowly, clutching the folio to her chest. The leather was cold, the scent of oil and aged parchment rising as she tightened her grip. She hadn't even heard the door open before he was between them.

And behind her, a voice said, low and smug, "I was hoping you'd come here."

⟫⟪

MARY-ANN TURNED, THE lantern trembling in her grip.

Rodney stepped from the shadows near the door, his boots quiet on the rotting floorboards. His coat was immaculate, his smile anything but. "It's unfortunate, really," he said, glancing at the folio in her hands. "You always were cleverer than you let on."

Her fingers curled tighter around the leather. "You knew I'd come."

"I knew you wouldn't be able to leave it alone. You were

born with too much curiosity—and too much pride." His eyes dropped to the documents. "You should hand those over now. They weren't meant for you."

"No," she said, her voice cold. "They were meant to destroy everything I love."

Rodney sighed, as if she'd disappointed him. "You don't understand what you've wandered into. You think this is about your father's company? About me?" He took a step closer. "This is bigger than all of us. It always has been."

"Then why hide it?" she said, lifting the folio slightly. "Why erase Quinton? Why fake ledgers and forge alliances and send a man to die?"

That wiped the smugness from his face. For a moment. Then he moved. Fast.

He lunged across the space between them, grabbing for the folio. Mary-Ann twisted away, but he caught her wrist, yanking her backward hard enough to send her shoulder into the crates. The lantern fell, rolling away with a metallic clatter.

"Give it to me," he hissed.

She shoved him with her free hand. "You'll never lay a hand on another Seaton ledger again."

He lunged toward her, fury flashing hot in his eyes. She stepped back, stumbling as her heel caught on a crate and sent her off balance. She hit the floor hard, her palm scraping against the wood. The folio skidded out of reach, landing several feet away.

Rodney bent for it. And was wrenched backward with such force he barely made a sound before crashing into the crates.

Quinton. He stood between them now, breathing hard, his fists clenched.

Rodney staggered upright, blood on his lip. "This doesn't concern you."

"It concerns me," Quinton said darkly, "more than you'll ever comprehend."

Rodney lunged again, but Quinton met him head-on this time, his blows brutal, fast, and unrelenting. The fight was nothing polished or strategic, just fury and fists, and three years of silence turned into motion. Crates splintered, dust choked the air, and Mary-Ann scrambled for the folio, cradling it to her chest as the men crashed against the far wall.

Rodney struck low. Quinton caught his elbow, turned, and drove him back again. It ended in seconds with Rodney groaning, pinned beneath Quinton's knee, his arm twisted behind him.

"You're done," Quinton said, breathing hard. "You won't touch her. Not this company. Not a single thing bearing the Seaton name."

The warehouse door opened sharply.

Barrington stood in the entrance, flanked by two men. His eyes swept the room in a moment and found Rodney on the floor, Quinton standing over him, Mary-Ann clutching the folio in the far shadows.

"We'll take him," Barrington said.

Quinton stepped back without a word. The other men moved in, hauling Rodney to his feet. He didn't fight now, he just laughed, low and bitter, wiping blood from his mouth.

As they pulled him past, he looked at Quinton and muttered, "You should've stayed gone."

Quinton didn't move. "And you should've known better than to underestimate her, especially a woman who keeps records."

Mary-Ann stepped next to Quinton and said, "Records that list every lie, every payment, and yes, even every name."

Rodney's smirk faltered.

Barrington met Mary-Ann's gaze and gave a single, respectful nod. "Well done."

Then they were gone. The echo of their steps faded, but the gravity of what had passed lingered, sharp, irrevocable, and finally hers to hold.

Silence returned like a tide.

The warehouse seemed larger without Rodney's presence, the air colder now that the immediate danger had passed. Mary-Ann stood where she was, the folio still pressed to her chest, her hands aching from the force of her grip.

Quinton turned toward her slowly. His knuckles were scraped raw. A cut bled along his temple. But his eyes, his eyes were only on her.

"Are you hurt?" he asked, voice low.

She shook her head. "You came."

"I had to."

Her lips trembled, but she said nothing.

He took a cautious step closer. "I didn't know. About the Order. About the plans. I thought… I thought I was a casualty of war. But I wasn't, was I?"

Mary-Ann released a shaky breath and offered him the folio. "They planned it. Your capture. Everything. To get you out of the way. So Rodney could take over. So I would—"

She couldn't finish.

Quinton didn't look away as he took the folio. He opened to the chart, then the report. His shoulders stiffened as he read.

"They erased me," he murmured. His hands shook. Three years lost. And all of it planned. "Like I was never meant to return."

She looked at him then, truly looked. "That's what they do."

He closed the folio with care. "They wanted to rewrite your future. They didn't count on you rewriting it back."

Mary-Ann blinked. "You believed in me once. Then you stopped."

"I didn't stop." His voice caught. "I buried it. Because I thought it was the only way to protect you. But I was wrong."

She waited.

Quinton stepped forward again, slow and sure. "I'll never ask you to stand aside. Or to be silent. If we do this, if we face what's left, it will be together. On your terms."

Her throat burned.

He reached for her hand, gently. "Say the word, and I'll walk away. But if you still want me—"

"I do," she whispered.

He nodded once. "Then I'm yours. No more lies. No more orders. Just us."

She didn't speak. But this time, she didn't let go of his hand.

She thought of every time she'd waited for him, every silence she'd endured. This wasn't the reunion she'd once imagined. But it was honest. It was hers. And she wasn't letting go.

Chapter Thirty-Three

IT WAS FRIDAY, and calm had returned to Sommer-by-the-Sea. The lamps in Barrington's study burned low, casting long golden shadows across the leather-bound reports on his desk. Outside, night still clung to the windows, though morning could not be far. Mary-Ann sat opposite Barrington, the folio between them, its red ribbon frayed but untouched.

She had not removed her gloves. Not since the warehouse. Not since Rodney.

Quinton stood at her side, arms crossed, jaw tight. He had refused to leave her side from the moment they'd left the dock.

Barrington's fingers moved over the first page, his eyes narrowing as he turned each sheet. "These are real," he said finally. "And dangerous."

Mary-Ann nodded once. "There's a forged partnership agreement near the back. It was meant to force my father's hand. To legitimize Rodney's control."

Quinton added, "The Order needed Seaton Shipping clean on paper. That's why they never named Mr. Seaton in any of the smuggling."

Barrington looked up. "They were going to blackmail him."

Mary-Ann's voice was quiet. "Until they had no need to."

He closed the folio with deliberate care. "You've struck a blow, Miss Seaton. And a hard one. There's panic in the Order's higher ranks. This was misplaced, you see."

She frowned. "Misplaced?"

Barrington gave a single nod. "According to our man inside, the Order's been looking for this folio before Quinton returned. No one knew who had it."

At that, Quinton looked at Mary-Ann.

Her fingers brushed over the ribbon once more. "It wasn't chance I found it."

Barrington studied her. Then he sat back. "Two arrests were made last night. Men we've been trying to identify for months. One is still in government. The other recently retired from the military. Rathbone and Trent."

"Will it be enough?" Quinton asked.

"No. But it's more than we've had in years." Barrington paused. "And it was your doing. Both of you."

Quinton's gaze flicked to Mary-Ann, his mouth softening. Pride, relief, and something long-buried, hope, perhaps, shone in his expression. He had seen her walk into fire. And win.

Mary-Ann didn't look away. "This isn't over."

He nodded once, solemn. "Then let's see it through.

THE SMALL MEETING room at Seaton Shipping had never felt so full.

Mr. Seaton sat at the head of the long table, his expression unreadable as the final pages of the folio were passed from hand to hand. Around the table sat three long-time associates of the company, gentlemen who had known her father since before Mary-Ann could walk, and one man from the Town Council, his seal case resting on the table beside him.

Mary-Ann stood beside her father, silent, her hands clasped behind her back. She had not spoken yet. She did not need to.

The Councilman cleared his throat. "This is sufficient. The ledger forgeries alone are damning, and the partnership document..." He shook his head. "It's plain fraud. There is no cause for further inquiry."

One of the merchants leaned forward. "So Seaton Shipping's name is restored?"

The Councilman gave a solemn nod. "Officially and without condition."

The words did not echo, but they landed heavily, and Mary-Ann felt the shift as if the building itself exhaled.

Her father leaned back, looking older than he had hours before, but there was something else, too. A quiet breaking in his expression. As if a long-held shame had finally lifted.

"I owe my daughter more than I can ever repay," he said, voice low but clear. "This company stands today because she refused to let it fall."

Mary-Ann glanced down, overwhelmed.

"You were right," he said, now looking at her. "About Rodney. About everything. I should have seen it sooner."

"You trusted the wrong man," she said gently. "But never for the wrong reasons."

The room was quiet a moment longer before the meeting was declared adjourned.

As the others filed out, Mr. Seaton reached for her hand, not with formality, but with fierce, fatherly pride.

There had been a time, not long ago, when she would have given anything for a word of approval. Now, it came without condition. Earned. Equal.

"I never thought I'd see the day," he murmured.

She smiled faintly. "Neither did I."

MARY-ANN FOLDED THE final page of the folio and placed it in the inner drawer of her father's desk. Her pulse had steadied. Her path was clear now.

A soft knock sounded at the door.

"Come in."

Lydia stepped into the study with her usual poise, but something in her expression faltered when she met Mary-Ann's gaze.

"You asked for me, Miss Seaton?" Lydia said, eyes flicking toward the desk, the window, anywhere but Mary-Ann's face.

"Yes." Mary-Ann gestured toward the chair. "You won't be staying."

Lydia blinked. "I... I don't understand."

"I believe you do," Mary-Ann said quietly. "Rodney is gone. And whatever arrangement he made on your behalf no longer exists."

Lydia didn't sit. Her jaw tightened. "I served this household faithfully."

"You spied on it," Mary-Ann corrected. "And I allowed it, because I needed to see just how deep his reach extended."

There was a long silence.

Then Lydia exhaled through her nose. "He wouldn't have helped me, would he? Even if I'd needed it."

Mary-Ann didn't answer. She didn't need to.

Lydia's expression flickered. She glanced toward the hall, then back again. "You should know... the folio," she said slowly. "It went missing months ago." No one knew where it was. Not even the ones giving orders."

Mary-Ann's breath caught. "You're certain?"

"I was told to search your room. I did. But it was already gone." Lydia hesitated. "They were desperate to recover it. Desperate enough to wonder if one of their own had turned."

Mary-Ann crossed to the desk and opened the drawer. Her fingers brushed the ribbon securing the folio.

"I found your name," she said softly. "*LF has served her purpose. The girl suspects nothing. Remove her quietly.*"

Lydia went still.

"I thought you should know what they planned," Mary-Ann added, voice still gentle. "So that you might plan something else."

Lydia didn't speak. When she finally did, her voice was low.

"I don't care who wins. But I'd rather not be on the losing side."

Mary-Ann studied her for a moment. "Then give me something."

Lydia's voice lowered. "They meet on the last Friday of every month. St. Andrew's Club. It's quiet. Private. Not everyone uses their real name."

Mary-Ann nodded once. "Thank you."

Lydia swallowed. "Will I be arrested?"

"No," Mary-Ann said simply. "But you won't be trusted. Not again."

Lydia gave a single nod and turned to go. Just before she reached the door, she looked back. "You're not the girl he thought you were."

Mary-Ann held her gaze. "No. I'm not."

Lydia's voice was quiet. "You're stronger." She paused and took a breath. "And smarter." She turned to leave.

"Lydia," Mary-Ann said softly. "As a parting gift, you may keep the dressing case."

Lydia blinked, the briefest trace of emotion passing over her face. Then she nodded, grateful, but quiet. She left without another word.

The door clicked shut.

Mary-Ann stood still for a moment, her hand resting on the back of the chair Lydia had never used. The silence settled around her, not empty, but earned. They had underestimated her. All of them.

She whispered, "Thank you, Hamish," and turned toward the window, where the evening light had just begun to shift.

Outside, the lamps had already been lit along the lane. Mary-Ann drew on her gloves, the folio now locked away, and turned her steps toward Sommer Chase, where the future she had once planned was waiting to be reclaimed.

Chapter Thirty-Four

IT WAS FRIDAY evening, and the wind off the sea carried the scent of salt and coming dusk. Mary-Ann arrived at Sommer Chase just as the lamps along the drive were being lit, her gloves still in hand and the hem of her cloak lifting with each step. The house rose ahead of her in warm silhouette, its windows glowing, not with grandeur, but with welcome.

She paused at the threshold, her hand resting lightly against the frame. This place had once belonged only to Barrington. To the Brigade. To causes larger than herself. But now it welcomed her too—not as an outsider, but as someone who had earned her place within its walls.

Inside, she found Quinton and Barrington in the study. The lamps had been extinguished, and the tall windows stood open to the soft spring air. The men sat comfortably but alert, the weight of unfinished business still resting between them.

No words were spoken at first. The folio had been reviewed. Agreements, quiet and firm, had been made. There was nothing more to explain.

Then, without warning, the front door opened, and Mrs. Bainbridge breezed in as though summoned by fate itself.

"I've done it," she declared, sailing into the room with a folded invitation in one hand and a triumphant expression on her face. "We've settled on a date. Barrington and I are to be married in September, the Saturday following The Masked Ball at Ravenshade."

Quinton blinked. Barrington looked up slowly from his chair.

"You've chosen a date," he repeated flatly.

Mrs. Bainbridge dropped a kiss onto his brow. "It was either that or let your mother do it, and frankly, I prefer civil war to ducal meddling."

Mary-Ann, still seated near the window, let out a breath of laughter. "Does this mean the list is final?"

"Heavens, no," Mrs. Bainbridge replied. "But the date is. And I've only told your father, the duchess, my aunt, the bishop, and three out of four of your groomsmen."

Barrington sighed. "I assume I'll be informed of the venue at some point."

"If you behave," she said sweetly, then turned to Mary-Ann. "Darling, will you help me choose the fourth groomsman?" Barrington keeps suggesting men who've been shot at."

"And survived," Barrington added mildly.

Mary-Ann smiled as their banter carried through the room. It was absurd and lovely, and for the first time in weeks, the air didn't feel heavy with decisions. It felt full of life again.

➤➤➤◄◄◄

LATER, AFTER THE house had quieted and the last bit of light slipped from the horizon, Mary-Ann stepped out into the gardens behind Sommer Chase.

The air was still, sweet with the scent of early spring blossoms and the faint tang of the tide. She wandered the path slowly, her hands bare now, the ache in her chest finally quiet. The roses had not yet bloomed, but new shoots were pushing through the soil, stubborn and sure.

A month ago, she would have doubted everything, her instincts, her courage, her worth. Now, she moved with certainty. Not because the danger had passed, but because she had *endured* *it.*

Footsteps approached behind her, soft but deliberate. She smiled, knowing it was Quinton.

He said nothing at first. He simply joined her, his coat unbuttoned, his expression open. The fading light softened the lines at his brow and warmed the curve of his jaw.

"How is your father?" he asked quietly.

"He's recovering," she replied. "He is a proud man. Rodney really fooled him about the business and about me. He knows the truth now. And he sees me. Really sees me. I'm even getting better at asking for help. Even Professor Tresham was helpful in the end," she added with a soft laugh. "Though I'm not certain he meant to be."

He nodded. "And Lydia?"

"She's gone. To some extent, she was just as much a tool of the Order as I was," she said. "Lydia left a few bruises, but no scars I can't live with."

They stood together, the hush between them no longer filled with uncertainty.

"I've been wondering something. The folio, why was it left behind? It seems too valuable for carelessness."

Mary-Ann reached into her pocket and drew out a folded scrap of paper. She didn't hand it to him. She read it aloud with a steady voice.

"*I knew you would find this. Keep it safe. — H.*"

Quinton's breath caught. "Hamish."

She nodded. "I think he was trying to tell me on the docks. I didn't understand at the time."

Quinton closed his eyes for a moment. "He saved your life twice, didn't he? Once when he pulled you out of the way. And again with that folio."

She looked down at the note, a whisper of a tear slipping free. "He would always hide sweets for me in the old warehouse when I was a girl." He used to say, '*ink on your nose*' when I got close to finding it, just to tease me." She smiled faintly. "That day..." she hesitated, her voice catching slightly. Then she went on. "I thought he said 'pity London.' But it was 'PT London.' He was trying to lead me to it."

Quinton took her hand, his fingers folding gently around hers. "He trusted you to finish what he couldn't."

"I was angry," she said softly. "At you. For not telling me what you knew. But I'm more angry at myself… for thinking you didn't believe in me."

"I believed in you," he said. "I always did."

She looked up, her gaze fierce and shining. "Then let's never let anyone do that to us again. Let's never let the world come between us."

He cupped her face with one hand, reverent. "I vow to never doubt you again. Never stand to stand beside you in silence when I should stand with truth. I vow to love you fiercely, and without condition."

She reached for him, pressing her hand over his heart. "And I vow to love you. Not as I once did. But as I do now, fully, and with eyes wide open."

Their kiss was quiet. Not rushed. Not desperate. Just two souls meeting where the wounds had once been and finding something stronger in their place.

When they pulled apart, Mary-Ann rested her forehead against his. "You came back changed," she said softly. "But so did I."

He smiled. "Then we'll learn each other again."

They stood like that for a long moment, wrapped in stillness. No audience. No vows witnessed. Just the truth.

He took her hand once more, his fingers strong and steady. Not anchoring her. Standing beside her.

And when they turned back toward the house, it wasn't the past they carried.

It was the future they had reclaimed, together.

The End

About the Author

There was never a time when *USA Today* Bestseller, RUTH A. CASIE hasn't had a story in her head. When she was little, she and her older sister would dress up and act out the ones Ruth creative. Today, Ruth writes exciting and beautifully told legendary historical romances that are both rich and engaging. Her stories feature strong women and the men who deserve them, endearing flaws and all. Her stories are full of, 'edge of your seat' suspense, mind-boggling drama, and a forever-after romance.

She lives in New Jersey with her hero, three empty bedrooms and a growing number of incomplete counted cross-stitch projects. Before she found her voice, she was a speech therapist (pun intended), client liaison for a corrugated manufacturer, and vice president at an international bank where she was a product/ marketing manager, but her favorite job is the one she's doing now—writing romance. Ruth hopes her stories become your favorite adventure.

Fun facts about Ruth:

1. She filled her passport up in one year.
2. She has three series. The Druid Knight is a time travel romance. The Stelton Legacy is a historical fantasy about the seven sons of a seventh son. Havenport Romances are contemporary romantic suspense stories. She also writes for the Pirates of Britannia connected world.
3. She did a rap with her son to "How Many Trucks Can a Tow Truck Tow If a Tow Truck Could Tow Trucks."

4. When she cooks she dances around the kitchen.

5. Her sudoku books is in the bathroom and that's all she'll
    say about that!

Social Media Links:

Website:
ruthacasie.com

Instagram:
instagram.com / ruthacasie

Facebook private reader's page, Casie Café:
facebook.com / groups / 963711677128537

Facebook Author Page:
facebook.com / RuthACasie

Twitter:
twitter.com / RuthACasie

BookBub:
bookbub.com / authors / ruth-a-casie

Amazon:
amazon.com / author / ruthacasie

Goodreads:
goodreads.com / author / show / 4792909.Ruth_A_Casie

YouTube:
bit.ly / 3hI5eQr